~ NIGHTMARES OF A HUSTLA ~

King Dream

Lock Down Publications and Ca$h
Presents
NIGHTMARES OF A HUSTLA
A Novel by *King Dream*

Lock Down Publications
P.O. Box 944
Stockbridge, Ga 30281

Visit our website @
www.lockdownpublications.com

Copyright 2020 King Dream
NIGHTMARES OF A HUSTLA

This is a work of fiction. Names, characters, places, and incidents either are products of the author's imagination or are used fictitiously. Any similarity to actual events or locales or persons, living or dead, is entirely coincidental.

Lock Down Publications
Like our page on Facebook: Lock Down Publications @
www.facebook.com/lockdownpublications.ldp
Cover design and layout by: **Dynasty Cover Me**
Book interior design by: **Shawn Walker**
Edited by: **Shamika Smith**

Stay Connected with Us!

Text **LOCKDOWN** to 22828 to stay up-to-date with new releases, sneak peaks, contests and more...
Thank you.

Submission Guideline.

Submit the first three chapters of your completed manuscript to ldpsubmissions@gmail.com, subject line: Your book's title. The manuscript must be in a .doc file and sent as an attachment. Document should be in Times New Roman, double spaced and in size 12 font. Also, provide your synopsis and full contact information. If sending multiple submissions, they must each be in a separate email.

Have a story but no way to send it electronically? You can still submit to LDP/Ca$h Presents. Send in the first three chapters, written or typed, of your completed manuscript to:

LDP: Submissions Dept
P.O. Box 944
Stockbridge, Ga 30281

DO NOT send original manuscript. Must be a duplicate.

Provide your synopsis and a cover letter containing your full contact information.

Thanks for considering LDP and Ca$h Presents.

Dedicated to: My Mother, Latonya "Boss Lady" Anderson

King Dream

~CHAPTER 1~

The walls in the tiny interrogation room seem to be closing in on Baby Red as the FEDs speak. All the guns and dope they found him along with surveillance videos of him serving weight to some undercover agents, he knew he was done for.

"We have enough evidence on you, Reddrick, to put your twenty-two-year-old ass away until Alzheimer's kicks in," Agent Briggs tells him. Baby Red leans back in his chair and folds his arms across his chest.

"I don't give a fuck, you Danny Devito looking motha-fucka. I've done time before. This shit ain't nothing new to me."

"You did time in juvey and two years in a soft ass Wisconsin minimum custody prison. This ain't a State case. You trafficked guns and drugs across state lines, so that makes this a Federal case. That means yo' ass is going to do FED time in a federal prison where them boys in the FEDs play by totally different rules. Rape and murder are as common in the federal prisons as finding candy in a fat kid's pocket. Don't think you'll be around a bunch of your homies from the block either. You see federal inmates get shipped out of state, so you'll be around a bunch of unsavory characters from all over the United States. Yo lil soft ass wouldn't last a day," Agent Evans tells him as he sparks a cigarette. Baby Red starting to feel those walls closing in more. Agent Evans blows out a cloud of Newport smoke in Baby Red's face.

"But it's something you can do to save yourself."

"What?"

"It's a few people you can get close to that we haven't been able to get within ten feet. You help us get the evidence we need on them and all the evidence we have on you will disappear. You'll be free to walk."

"Yo, I ain't no fucking snitch!"

"The way I see it is you either be a snitch or prepare to be somebody's bitch. Those your only two choices. Think about that tonight while you're sitting in your cell."

"Take my card. If you decide to change your mind give me a call," Agent Briggs says, setting the card down in front of him.

After changing over into the standard orange inmate uniform, Baby Red is escorted to his pod. Inside the pod was a whole other world. The pod was setup with two tiers, a top one and a lower one. Each tier had thirty cells on it. The whole setting had a warehouse-like floorplan. In the middle of the pod were two Dayrooms, one on the left side and one on the right. Each Dayroom had seven sets of blue plastic couch like chairs and a 42" flat screen television. Behind the Dayroom sat the dining area were three rows of five tables and their four chairs accompanied. Behind the dining area were the phone trees. Two poles that housed six phones each. One phone tree sat on the right side of the room and one sat on the left side. Behind that was the guards' station. On the far right of the guards' station was three shower stalls. The far left of the guards' station was three more shower stalls. Behind the guards' station were windows and a door that lead to the gym.

As Baby Red walked into the room, all eyes locked on him. He kept a grim look on his face. If he learned anything so far from being locked up in juvey and minimum-security prison, it was even if you are scared, you better not show it. Niggas in the joint are like wolves, they can sense fear and will prey on you.

His escort walks him over to the guard's station to get logged in. "Walton, you're in cell B-9." The pudgy, redheaded, female guard told him. Baby Red walked over to his cell. He sees the bottom bunk was already occupied by somebody. He puts his stuff on the top bunk and begins making his bed. Moments later, a buff dark-skinned dude walks in the cell.

"Nigga, what the fuck you doing in my room?"

Damn, I ain't even had time to make a shank, is all that ran through Baby Red's mind before he turned around.

"Mothafucka-" he begins to say as he turned around to face his newest enemy. But when he saw the man that was confronting him, he cut his sentence short. "Wild Boy Billy mothafuck'n Gunz? What it do baby?" Billy Gunz flashed a smile that showed a mouth full of gold and diamonds. Baby Red shakes his hand and embrace him in a half hug.

"Fool, I heard you were here, so I had my inside connect send you over here to cell up with me."

"Oh, you got some inside connects huh?"

"Of course." Billy Gunz pulls a cellphone out of his mattress and tosses it to Baby Red. "That's what that money do. Put the towel up over the door window when you use it, so they'll think you taking a shit. When you done making your calls, slide it back in the mattress then come out and holla at me."

"Cool." They shake hands and Billy Gunz walks back out into the day room. Billy Gunz was one of the big homies in the hood who made plenty of money from hustling. With his foreign cars, foreign women, expensive clothes, and jewelry made him one of Baby Red's greatest hood idols. They called him Wild Boy Billy Gunz because he was always about that action. He didn't care where he was or who you were if you got out of line, he was coming from the waist with two pistols like Billy The Kid.

Baby Red put the towel over the door's window and proceeded to make a call to his homeboy Wee Wee. "Yo, who dis?"

"Nigga, this Baby Red."

"Oh shit! What up, my nigga? Mothafuckas talking about you got knocked. Where the fuck you at?"

"I did get knock. The FEDs got me, my nigga."

"What happens?"

"The shit was crazy, man. I go meet up with Spooky in Minnesota to drop off four ounces and some guns to him. I come out of the spot and the FEDs were everywhere."

"That nigga Spooky set you up."

"Naw, it wasn't him because that nigga came out busting and went out in a blaze of glory. The shit was like a scene in a movie."

"Damn! R.I.P. to a real nigga."

"Yea, he went out like a G. I wouldn't finna go out like that though. I'd rather be judged by twelve than to be carried by six. You feel me?"

"Yea, but what you going to do now? You know when the FEDs got a mothafucka, they got him dead to rights. It's hard to get out their chokehold."

"I heard. I got a lil bread put up. I'm going to grab a lawyer and see what's good."

"Alright, hit me back let me know what's good. Keep yo head up in there and leave the soap on the floor my nigga."

"Yea, yea." He ends the call and just before he makes his next call there's a knock at the door.

"Walton, what's going on in there? Why is your window covered?" the redhead guard asks as she makes her rounds.

"I'm taking a shit!"

"Just making sure you're okay in there." She walks off and he continues making his next call.

"Hello!"

"What's up beautiful?"

"Don't what's up me. Why you ain't come home last night or been answering your phone? People talking about you got locked up, but I see that's a lie seeing there ain't no operator patching this call through. So, what bitch you with?"

"Damn. Paris, take a breath. I ain't with no bitch and wasn't with one. Look, baby, the FEDs knocked me yesterday in Minnesota. They got me down here on some serious drug and gun trafficking charges."

"Are you serious?"

"Yea and they killed Spooky."

"Oh my God!"

"Listen, I need you to call that super lawyer that had got your cousin Jerry off his FED charges."

"Robert Dingles?"

"Yea, call him and tell him to come see me asap."

"I got you." The guard does another round and stops at his cell. She knocks on the door.

"Yo, I'm coming out right now!" He flushes the toilet and he could see her silhouette walk away from the door.

"I got to go. I'll call you later." He hangs up the phone and slides it back into the hiding spot. He walks out into the busy day room. He spots Billy Gunz sitting at one of the dining tables playing chess with another cat. He walks over and pulls up a seat.

"You handled yo' business, lil dawg?" Billy Gunz asks as he moves his knight from 22 to 37, taking his opponent's pawn and threatening his queen on 54.

"Yea, I had my bitch hit up Robert Dingles for me. I'm gonna see what that fool says when he comes to see me. Hopefully, he can find a loophole or something because I don't see no way out of this one," Baby Red says, rubbing his face.

"As long as there's a way in, there's always a way out." His opponent moves his queen to 38 and threatens his bishop.

"Yea, well, the way out the FEDs offering is not a real nigga's avenue and I'm definitely not interested in traveling down that road."

"They trying to initiate you into their snitch clique, huh? Telling you why do ten years, when you can tell on a friend?" he says with one finger on his chin as he studies the board.

"Hell yea. But I'm too real for that shit, my nigga. I'd rather do my time than to ever drop a dime on mine. You know what I mean?"

"I feel you. Why sacrifice the whole empire just to save yourself." His opponent was so occupied with trying to take his knight that threatened his queen that he forgot about the pawn Billy Gunz had on 55 that was threatening his rook. He takes the rook and turns his pawn into a queen.

"Damn! I forgot about that damn pawn," his opponent says as he claims the bitter prize of Billy Gunz's knight on 37 with his queen.

"And I see you still don't see the big picture." He moves his bishop from 62 to 26 leaving his opponent nowhere for his king to escape to. "Checkmate." His opponent studies the board a few moments in search of a way out but finds nowhere to retreat.

"Damn! Let's run it again."

"Maybe later, right now I need to holla at my mans." Billy Gunz jerks his head to the left telling Baby Red to follow him. They walk through the gym doors and into the gym. The gym was nothing more than a full basketball court. Five men were playing a game of hustle basketball when they walked in. Billy Gunz and Baby Red chose to walk laps around the court. "So, what happened? How you get knocked?" Baby Red broke down the same story to him that he gave Wee Wee.

"What you think? I'm done for, right?"

"That boy Robert Dingles is a beast. I know a few cats with worse cases than yours he got off scot-free. If you get him like you said you are, then sit back and let him work his magic. You'll be home in no time."

"I hope you right. What you doing in here though?"

"You know I'm on FED papers for that dope case I caught a few years back."

"Yea, yea, I remember. That's when they caught you with those bricks here in Minnesota."

"Yea. My probation officer hit me with a sanction for leaving town without permission."

"What you needed a vacation, my nigga?"

"Nah, I had a connect down in Atlanta that had some straight drop, no cut, for the low. I had to get my hands on that. Especially with all this bullshit dope floating around here. So, I jumped in my Benz and had my white bitch follow me down there in her minivan. I loaded twelve bricks into her shit. A professional-looking white bitch with two small white kids in a soccer van. I knew I wouldn't have any problems getting that work back to the Mil."

"So, what went wrong?"

"The dope made it back safely. But leaving Georgia, a bitch ass state trooper pulled me over for failure to signal. When I went to see my PO last week, she had already been notified that I had got pulled over in Tennessee and had a pair of cuffs waiting on my black ass. Hit me with a hundred-twenty days sanction."

"That ain't too bad. At least you know that you're going home. I still got to go in front of the judge with my fingers cross and clutching a crucifix."

"You going home soon too, nigga." The ball the men were playing hustle with got away from them and rolled over to

Billy Gunz. He picks the ball up and shoots a three-point basket from where he stood. The ball hits the backboard and falls
into the basket. The men hustle for the rebound. Billy Gunz
turns his attention back to Baby Red. "The question is, what
are you going to do when you get out?"

"Get back to the money. I know with the bread it's going
to cost to hire Robert Dingles, I'm going to be tapped for cash.
So, I'm going to go to my mans, Baggy. I'll have him front
me about four and a half ounces to get back on my feet."

"Yea right. Baggy can't loan you no four and a split."

"What you mean? That's my mans, I know he got it and
he knows I'm good for it."

"You must ain't heard."

"Heard what?"

"I guess word travels faster in here than it does out there.
Some niggas caught Baggy slipping the other day. Ran up in
his house took all his shit and smoked his fool ass."

"They killed Baggy?"

"Hell yea. I guess you got to find you a new plug." They
walked a few more laps reminiscing about people and events
that happened in the hood before returning to their cells for
count.

~ CHAPTER 2 ~

The next morning, Baby Red was standing in front of his sink washing his face when the guard came to his door. "Walton, you have an attorney visit. Be ready in five minutes to be escorted."

Baby Red walks into a small room where a white man with blonde hair and a tailored blue Armani suit. "Mr. Walton, please take a seat. I'm Robert Dingles," he says as he shakes his hand. "Your girlfriend, Paris, called me to come see you." Baby Red takes a seat in front of Robert.

"Did you take a look at my case?"

"I did. And from what I've read, any attorney will tell you that your goose is cooked." Baby Red drops his head in defeat. Robert takes a drink of water from the glass that sat on the table. "But I'm not just any attorney. I'm the best. From what I see, you certainly have a fighting chance." Baby Red raised his head at the newfound hope.

"You can beat this case?"

"I can beat it. I'm so sure I can beat this case that if I don't, I'll give you every dime of your money back."

"How much are we talking?"

"If it doesn't have to go to trial, eight thousand. If it does, twenty-five thousand. But I strongly doubt that it would. If you want to hire me, I will be needing a five-thousand-dollar retainer. So, what do you say?"

"I say let's do this! I'll have Paris drop the whole eight thousand off to you today."

"And as soon as she does, I'll be all over this case. In the meantime, do the DA no favors. Keep quiet. Don't talk to the police, other inmates, or anyone. Remember loose lips sink ships."

Baby Red left the visit with a smile on his face. He called Paris and told her to drop the money off to Dingles and then he went looking for Billy Gunz to tell him what happened at his visit. He found him sitting with two other men on the left side day room watching "The First 48". Baby Red takes a seat next to Billy Gunz. "I got twenty noodles, five bags of chips, three Snickers, and a bag of coffee that says the nigga get to telling."

"Hell naw, Billy. That nigga is solid. Look how he carries himself. Like a true killer. That nigga ain't finna tell them fags shit."

"If you are so confident, Joey Long, then put yo money where your money where yo mouth is."

"Alright. But fuck them zu-zus and wham-whams. I got five G's that says the nigga don't speak."

"You ain't said nothing I can't handle. We on."

"Bet." The commercials ended and the show continued where it left off. A young nigga sat in a small Miami interrogation room. His face was fixed with a permanent mug. He looked like the type of nigga that will kill a mothafucka just because he's bored. As the detectives gently questioned him, he gave off that 'fuck you and don't fuck with me' attitude. The detectives were not getting anywhere, then they tried switching their tactics. "Now, you're insulting my intelligence by lying to my face! We know for a fact you knew the victim. We also have an eyewitness who says you and the victim had an altercation outside the club. We also have video footage of a gray Monte Carlo like yours pulling up to the victim's apartment building, and I bet we find your DNA inside that apartment. If I have to jump through all these hoops to get the truth, then you can forget all about making any deals or the courts showing you any mercy. I will make sure you're charged and convicted of capital murder. Now, Lil E are you going to tell me the truth, or am I going to have to jump through the loops?"

"Give that pig no help, Lil E. Make his bitch ass work for a conviction!" Joey Long yells at the TV.

"All that cheering you doing on the sideline ain't helping shit. This nigga finna break. You can see it in his eyes," Billy Gunz says. Billy Gunz and Joey long both watch closely as the moment of truth unfolds. Lil E stares at the table but you could tell what he was really doing was replaying the whole event in his head. The other detective in the room notices just that, so he made his move.

"Lil E, you didn't mean for all this to go down like it did, did you?" Lil E's bottom lip begins to quiver, and he shakes his head no before the tears began rolling down his face.

"There it is!" Billy Gunz yell.

"Yo ass bet not talk Lil E!" Joey long yells.

"I know deep down you are a good person, and this has been eating you up. It's eating up the victim's family too. Help them find peace by telling us what happened."

"Don't do it, Lil E! Lawyer up nigga!" Joey yells out.

Lil E wipes the tears from his face. "Me and the victim, Darnell, had some words in the club because I was fucking his baby mama and the nigga didn't like it. We got into a fight and the bouncers broke it up. We all got in our cars to leave and Darnell pulled up beside us flashing a gun. He said the next time he sees me, he busting on sight. So, I said I'm going to get him before he gets me."

"Then what happened?"

"Me, John John, and Pistol went to his apartment."

"John John is Johnathan Jones and Pistol is Markel Heights, right?"

"Yea."

"Okay, then what happened?"

"Pistol kicked the door in and -"

"Man, what the fuck? I don't even want to see no more. You won Billy. I thought this nigga was a killa. His bitch ass folded like a lawn chair."

"Joey Long, it's of no wonder why yo ass got knocked. You're a terrible judge of character. You've been in these streets long enough to know that sometimes these so-called killas be the first mothafuckas to snitch. Now, where's my money?"

"I'm finna call my bitch and have her put it on yo books now. But this shit ain't over. Don't forget we still got that bet on who gets sent home on *Big Brother* tonight."

"I ain't got no problem with taking some more of your money." Joey fans Billy off and goes to hop on the phone. "Baby Red, let's go for a stroll my nigga." They go into the empty gym and begin walking laps as they talked. "Dingles had any good news for you?"

"Did he? The nigga said he so sure he can beat it that he'll give me my money back if he doesn't."

"You know lawyers don't ever give guarantees like that, so that means he knows the FEDs fucked up somewhere and they ain't going to have no choice but to let you go. How much he whacking you?"

"Eight G's if I don't have to go to trial and twenty-five if I do. But he says he strongly doubt that we will have to go to trial."

"Like I said, he got the FEDs by the balls on this one. You got the bread to hire him?"

"Yea, I got my girl dropping it off to him right now."

"Then you're good. You going to go in front of the judge Monday and be home before dinner."

"You think so?"

"My nigga, I know so."

"I'm geeked and all but I still have one problem when I get home." Billy picks up a basketball and dribbles it as they walk.

"What's that?"

"With my money blown on this attorney and Baggy dead, I have no connect or way to re-up."

"So, what you going to do?"

"I was hoping you can front me a four and a split until I get on my feet." Billy stops walking and dribbling the ball. He looks Baby Red up and down.

"Take off your shirt."

"What?"

"Take off your shirt, nigga."

"What you think I'm wearing a wire or something?"

"Baby Red, I love you like a lil brother, nigga. But if you don't take off that shirt, I'm going to bust yo head wide open." Baby Red takes off his shirt and turns in a circle so Billy Gunz could see he wasn't wearing a wire.

"You satisfied? Can I put my shirt back on now?"

"Yea, I just had to make sure."

"You would think you know me better than to be a snitch."

"You ain't learn shit from watching *The First 48* a minute ago? I'm sure that lil nigga's friends John John and Pistol never thought he would be a snitch. I didn't make it this far in the game without being cautious. And when you reach this level in the game, you'll understand why it seems my caution crosses the line of paranoia." Baby Red puts his shirt back on and they continue walking.

"So, will you front me the work?"

"I don't know, Baby Red. You asking for a lot."

"Think about it? Come on, you just said I'm like a lil brother to you. Help lil bro get back on his feet. If four and a half ounces is asking too much, then just slide me two ounces. If the shit is as good as you say it is, I'll make it work."

"Like I said, I'll think about it. Right now, I got a poker game to play." Billy Gunz shoots a basket that bounced off the rim and hit the floor then he walked out the gym.

Baby Red laid on his bunk staring up at the ceiling, thinking while listening to Lil Poppa songs blast through Billy Gunz radio. Billy Gunz stood at the desk in their cell with his shirt off making jailhouse pizzas. For the last two days, Baby Red and Billy Gunz talked about a little of everything. Everything but what Baby Red really wanted to talk about. As much as he was tempted to bring up the idea of Billy Gunz fronting him some work, he didn't. He didn't want to agitate him. Billy Gunz was easily agitated when he felt pestered. And once he's agitated, what could've been a yes becomes a solid no followed by a mouth full of blood. However, tomorrow was his court day and with the high chances of him getting out, he felt no choice but to ask him again. "Say Billy Gunz, you know tomorrow I might be leaving and shit. And -" Billy Gunz without turning around holds up one finger and continues spreading the cheese on the pizzas. Then he turned down the radio.

"Sliding you the work ain't no problem. The issue that worries me is mingling the lines of friends and business. You see I'm ruthless when it comes to my money Baby Red. And nor friends or family is an exception to my wrath when I'm crossed. I don't take no shorts or no losses, and my money better always be on time. And since I'm doing you a favor you got to do me one in return." Billy Gunz said, already knowing what Baby Red wanted to talk about.

"What you need?"

"I'm losing money every second I'm sitting in this bitch and it's making me sick. I need you to handle my business for me while I'm in here. Do that and instead of fronting you a four and a split, I'll give you ten ounces out of every key you sell. If you can handle that, then we can do business."

"Hell yeah, I can handle that. I push weight like a body-builder. I'll make sure you have all your money and have it on time. So, how we going to do this?"

"Don't put the wagon in front of the horse. You've got to get out first. But for now, let's smash these pizzas." He passes Baby Red a medium size pizza overflowing with chunks of ground beef, peppers, and cheese.

Baby Red laid in bed trying to go to sleep, but he couldn't. No matter if he counted a million sheep while lying on a sleep number mattress, he couldn't fall asleep. He was too excited about all the possibilities that tomorrow will bring. As he laid in bed daydreaming, a guard taps on his door. He jumps up. "What up?"

"Walton, pack up. You're being released."

"Released?"

"Yea, all charges have been dropped." Baby Red jumped down and started cleaning his shit out as fast as he could.

"Look at you, ain't even got to step into a courtroom. I told you, Dingles had them mothafuckas by the balls," Billy Gunz says sitting up in the bed stretching and wiping the sleep from his eyes.

"I can't help but wonder what it was that saved my ass. I'll make sure to ask him when I talk to him," Baby Red says as he gathers his paperwork and threw all his other belongings in the garbage. Billy Gunz stood up, they shook hands and embraced each other in a half hug.

"Be easy out there, lil dawg. And don't trip; I'll have my people drop that off to you."

"Cool."

"Just remember what I said. Because you'll hate to make me yo enemy, Red."

"You ain't got nothing to worry about bruh. I got this."
Baby Red walks out of the cell and out of the jail a free man.

~ CHAPTER 3 ~

It's been almost a week now since Baby Red has been out and still no word from Billy Gunz. He's starting to feel like Billy Gunz was just jacking at the mouth about putting him on. Thinking he probably just told him that to keep him from bugging him. Regardless of all that, Baby Red needed to get back on and get back on fast. Between the four ounces he lost when the police raided Spooky's spot and the money he paid Dingles to get him out, he was broke. So broke that he now paces the floor in his kitchen contemplating whether or not he should rob Poky. Poky is the neighborhood weed man who sold his shit by the pound. He's one of the OG's on the block. He's known Baby Red since Baby Red was in pampers. Poky's a cool cat that'll always have a mothafucka laughing. But the jokes on you if you ever think for a second that the nigga is a pushover. He would never hesitate to put some hot ones in the nigga's ass who crosses him. Baby Red knew if he busts this move, he would have to kill Poky. As much as he didn't want to do it to the nigga who used to buy him and all the other kids in the neighborhood ice cream from the ice cream truck and give them a dollar every time he saw them, but he was hungry. And when a wolf gets hungry, everything moving is a meal on his menu.

Poky only dealt with a chosen few that faithfully bought six or seven pounds from him a week. He only dealt with those chosen few because he trusted them. He needed to only do business with people he trusts because Poky never took his money upfront. He didn't want his weed and money in the same place at the same time. He said he'd rather take a loss on one of them than a loss on both if the police or some niggas ever ran up on him. Baby Red knew from riding around with Poky as a kid soaking up game that today was the day that he collected all the money from the people he fronted pounds to. For Baby Red, it was no better day than today to make his move.

The streetlights were out but the moon gave what little light it had to the block. The block was deserted except for a couple of crackheads stealing the copper off the abandoned house that stood two houses from the corner. Baby Red dressed in all black with his hoodie and baseball cap drawn tight over his head along with a mask that only covered his face from the nose on down. He crouches down by some garbage cans in the alley behind Poky's house and ties the laces of his all-black Timberland boots and cocks back his twin Glocks. With a hunger for money rumbling in his gut, it was time to eat. But before he stood up, his phone rang. He hurries to turn it off, so he doesn't alert anybody but when he sees the unknown number, he decides to answer it.

"Hello."

"You figured out how Dingles got you out?"

"Billy Gunz?"

"Yea nigga, it's me."

"He said the video footage they had of me serving an undercover never showed my face and the undercover agent that I served was thrown off the force for illegal activities. They also found the guns and dope in Spooky's house and not on me, so they had nothing they could actually charge me with."

"Sounds about right to me. I bet you thought I was on some bullshit because I ain't hit you up yet." Baby Red abandons his mission and starts walking out the alley.

"I can't lie, I did think you were on some bullshit. I mean, it's been almost a week my nigga and I ain't heard shit from you."

"It's all about being cautious, Baby Red. You know how you call the weight man and tell him to bring you your re-up and he takes all day? Then when you call him back, he says he'll be pulling up in a minute and that he's right up the street, but it still takes him another hour to get to you? That's because he's practicing precaution. He's peeping the scene, making sure there's no surprises awaiting him. And if you going to be on this level of the game, you better start practicing these same precautions."

"I feel you."

"Good because Santa Claus just came down your chimney. Them presents are already at home waiting on you."

"Get the fuck out of here. You for real?"

"Yea, I'm for real, nigga. Go check it out and I'll call you back a lil later." Billy Gunz disconnects the call. Baby Red couldn't get to the house fast enough. His speed walking turned into a full-on sprint as he made his way to his doorstep. Coming in the house, he sees Paris sitting on the couch. She was talking on the phone to one of her homegirls about some other bitches the two them don't like.

"Yea girl, that bitch be thinking she killing shit with them basement made ass injections she walking around with." Baby Red walks over to her.

"Somebody drop something off for me?" She holds up one finger to him and continues running her mouth on the phone.

"Bitch, I know it's fake because Mona told me that they both got theirs done the same day by Freddy's gay ass in his basement. And my brother Chino said when he squeezed her ass the night she let him fuck, the shit felt hard like the hoe had Fixer Flat in her shit or something." Baby Red was feeling too anxious to have the patience Paris was asking for right then.

"Paris, you can talk about all bullshit later! Now, did a mothafucka drop something off for me or not?" Paris exhales a deep breath and rolls her eyes before getting up. With her caramel ass cheeks hanging out of her tight black boy shorts, she walks into the kitchen with the phone still to her ear. She opens up the oven door and pulls out a fully cooked turkey and handed him a card off the top of the refrigerator.

"This came with it." The card read:

'The turkey's good, but the stuffing is even better.'

He gives Paris a quick kiss on the lips.

"Thank you, baby."

"Umm-hmm, whatever," she says, rolling her eyes again and continuing her phone conversation as she walked out the kitchen.

Baby Red opens up the turkey and removes two fat kilos of coke. He quickly cleaned them off then opens one up. He dips his finger into it and tasted the powder. His tongue immediately went numb. He rubbed a little on his gums, grabbed a straw out the kitchen drawer, and then blew a line of it to test it out. "Oh shit! That shit fire. That's definitely getting cut. I'm back in business, baby," he says out loud to himself with a smile on his face.

Baby Red immediately went to work busting down the bricks. He cut them to stretch his profits even more, but not so much as to take too much potency out of the dope. He rocked some up and kept some soft for his powder head customers and the cats that like to cook their shit themselves. He slid Paris a quarter of an ounce to get off at the club where she dances. All her stripper friends were powder heads and some of her customers were too. As good as this dope is, he was sure she'll be calling him to drop her off some more before the end of the night. In the meantime, he hit up his customers and let them know he was back on deck with an even better supply. After getting a few of them started with a sample of the new shit, his phone start blowing up nonstop. He drops off an ounce of rock up to Wee Wee on the South Side to get off.

Wee Wee's Aunt Linda was one of the biggest crackheads on the South Side. She knew all the crackheads around and they all came to her house to smoke and get their dope. For a dime sack off every hundred we made, she let us serve out her house. That meant she would be hustling just as hard getting people to spend so she could stay high. It was a win-win situation for Baby Red.

Within eight days, Baby Red was down to his last three ounces. Billy Gunz didn't leave a number for Baby Red to contact him. Instead, Billy Gunz would call him every day or so to check up on things. Seeing how Billy Gunz moved, Baby Red put in for another order two days ago when he was down to less than half a brick. When he placed that order, Billy Gunz gave him instructions on where to drop off his money. He had him take it to a Catholic church on the West Side of town and leave it under the seat in the confession booth.

The shit was moving fast, and it was only a matter of time before those last three ounces were gone. Luckily Paris called him saying she got another package for him. This time it was dropped off to her at work in the form of a teddy bear followed by some roses and a card. A card that read:

They say it's what's in the inside that counts...

It was no surprise that the package showed up at her job. Everybody knew Paris was Baby Red's girl and that she was a stripper at Pole Queens Strip Club. He also knew Billy Gunz was practicing precaution again by not delivering to the same place twice in a row. He took the bear home and cut it open, removing four keys this time along with a note. The note read:

Now that I see how you move; I can trust you with my customers. Call them and tell them The Hills Are White This Time Of Year. They'll know what's up. I'll be in touch...

The paper had a list of thirteen names and phone numbers. Baby Red went to work calling each one. The last contact on the list didn't have a number listed, just an address. The address led him to a biker bar on the white side of town. He didn't have a good feeling about going in a bar where he was sure to be the only black face in there, so he slipped his twin Glocks in his waistband before walking in.

As soon as he entered, all conversations came to a halt and all eyes fell on him. An old German song played on the jukebox. A huge picture of Hitler hung on a wall by the pool table. Most of the men and women inside the bar sported leather biker vest that read Aryan Angels with an image of a motorcycle that had Swastika symbols for its rims. Billy Gunz had to have made a mistake on the info he sent him for this contact. To be sure, he swallowed hard and walked over to the bartender. "Aye. my mans. Tell me where I can find White Boy Nick." The big blue-eyed skinhead's face balled up into a mug.

"White Boy? Did you hear us call yo Black ass Boy when you walked yo tar skin ass in here?"

"Tar skin? Mothafucka, I'm only a few shades darker than yo pink ass. And the mothafucka I'm looking for calls himself White Boy Nick. Now, do you know his ass or not?" The bartender looks over at one of the men that stood by the door and nods his head. The man locks the door. Seeing this, Baby Red knew it was finna be some shit, so he clutched his twins.

"I don't like your tone hip hop. In fact, I feel offended by you, maybe even a little threatened." The other men in the bar start closing in on Baby Red. He pulls out his twins and at the same time, even more guns were pointed back at him. Another skinhead with a huge scar on the left side of his face stepped forward.

"What business do you have with White Boy Nick?"

"I just came to tell him the hills are white this time of year."

"Well shit, why you ain't say that in the first place? I'm White Boy Nick. Give me two ounces of that beautiful white Aryan bitch." Everyone put their guns away.

"I'll take one myself!" another man yells, then the majority of the bar begins shouting orders. Seeing all the tension die out, Baby Red put away his guns and got down to business. He had to have Paris bring him some more work from the crib to handle all the orders the Aryans made. After reluctantly having drinks with White Boy Nick, Baby Red found out a lot about him and the Aryan Nation. White Boy Nick was the owner of the bar and the leader of the Aryan Angels Biker Gang. His point of view on life was more different than Baby Red thought. It turned out the Aryan Angels weren't like the radical skinheads and Nazis that the majority of the world knew. The Aryan Angels didn't care about what color a person was when it came to friends and business. They believe there's beauty in all races. Their only discrimination when it came to race was preserving your own race by breeding with your own kind and taking pride in your people. Baby Red could see the logic in that. He couldn't see anything other than a Black woman by his side. Even though Paris is half Cuban, in the eyes of society and God, just a drop of that dominant Black gene still makes her a Black woman.

King Dream

~ CHAPTER 4 ~

Business has been booming. Baby Red's been receiving more orders than he could handle. He hadn't got more than a few hours of sleep a day since he first started booming. He sees the only way he could keep up with all the orders was to hire more workers, which lead him to recruit his cousin, Do-Dirty, along with Pay Pay and Noodles. Baby Red grew up with all of them. Do-Dirty is a good hustler, but he also has a tendency to be a hothead. Baby Red made the decision to keep him close by. He figured with a close eye on him it would keep him from wilding out. Pay Pay, he's the real antisocial type. The only language he speaks is money and if you ain't talking that then there'll be no conversation in progress. Baby Red copped a spot UptownUptown for him to work. Noodles, she's a dike bitch who everybody says look just like Chyna Whyte. She didn't take any shit from anybody. A mothafucka come at her sideways, she'll be quick to put them in their place by any means. Baby Red grabbed a spot on the West Side for her.

Now with his workload lighter, he had a little more free time to do other things. And the first thing he had in mind was to splurge a little.

Walking side by side with shopping bags in hand, Baby Red and Paris tear down the mall. "Did my baby get every-thing she wants?" Baby Red says, putting his arm around her.

"Nope."

"What didn't you get?" he inquires, looking at all the bags.

"I didn't get my name on the mall," she says, making them both laugh. A laughed that was short-lived when she sees who was walking their way. "Here comes Truth and Tokyo." Truth and Baby Red have known each other since middle school. They never had any real beef. They were just one of those cases where two people don't sync up. They never vibe because they were always in competition with each other ever since they've known one another. Paris and Tokyo share the same competitive attitude towards each other. They're both strippers at the same club and always trying to outdo each other in everything they do. Whether that be in hairstyles, clothes, shoes, nails, or getting money, they always had to try and top one another.

Paris and Tokyo's rivalry was more understandable. Tokyo is a fine ass Asian and Black bitch who was Baby Red's bitch before she got with Truth. Baby Red fucked off on Tokyo with Paris. When word of the affair got back to Tokyo, she snatched Paris off the pole at the club and they fought 'til the bouncers were forced to break them up. After that, they fought every time they saw each other for two months straight. But the same week Tokyo had got news of the affair, she jumped ship from Baby Red and got with Truth.

"Well if it isn't Baby Red 'Mr. Houdini' himself. I heard you slipped out of the FED's chokehold. What did that cost you? Or should I say who?" Truth says.

"You trying to insinuate that I told my way out? Let me tell you something, nigga. I ain't never been a snitch. I paid good money for the best mothafuckin' lawyer in this whole Midwest region to get me out. I don't fuck with snitches and I'll never be one. In fact, the only snitch I ever met in my life was you."

"I'm a real nigga and ain't never told on nobody."

"Wasn't you the one that told Tokyo about me fucking off with Paris? Nigga, if you would rat on a nigga for some pussy, I could only imagine the things you tell for the price of your freedom. I guess they really call you Truth because that's exactly what you swear to tell when you take the stand."

"What, Baby Red, you still sore about me leaving you for him?" Tokyo asks, but Paris chimes in before Baby Red could say a word.

"Bitch, he ain't thinking about yo plastic body ass. He fucked off with me because yo ass wasn't good enough. Speaking of ass, I see you bought another one. What is that? Complements of Freddie's basement injections?"

"Bitch, I-" Truth holds his hand out, stopping Tokyo from running up on Paris.

"Chill with all the extra shit and keep cool while I rap with Baby Red for a minute." Tokyo and Paris continued quietly arguing while Baby Red and Truth took a seat on a bench.

"What you want to rap about Truth?"

"Look, you and I ain't never seen eye to eye, but up until now we always had respect for each other."

"Up until now? What you mean?"

"You know it's an unspoken rule on the East Side about asking for permission before taking over a block."

"Hold up, you lost me. I don't even have a spot on the East Side. That's too close to home. The few customers I deal with on that side of town I have Do-Dirty Come to them."

"Well, Do-Dirty set up shop over on Richards and Locust at Eddie Cain's spot. You know that's my spot, right? I went and confronted him the other day and he upped the strap on me saying that you were taking over now. I know Do-Dirty is a hothead and he's your blood, so instead of sending my hittas to move him around or lay him down, I wanted to holla at you first and see if we could get an understanding."

"I'm going holla at Do-Dirty. But you know if something ever was to happen to my cousin, you could count two and three because it's been one. You know how I get down. I would light yo whole fucking world up."

"Yea, I know how you get down and you know how I get down. So, get an understanding with yo cousin, and let's not let this turn into a war neither one of us really want." Truth gets up from the bench and walks off. "Say bye to your friend, Tokyo. We out of here."

"Paris."

"Bitch," Paris replies. Truth and Tokyo walk off while Baby Red and Paris make their exit as well in the opposite direction. "What did his ass want?"

"Do-Dirty has been setting up shop at one of his spots and muscling him out."

"Bae, I told you that I had a bad feeling about yo cousin. I also told yo stupid ass not to put him on yo team," she says, hitting him in the arm with one of her shopping bags. "That nigga is too reckless. He ain't even been with you a whole month, yet and he's already getting some bullshit started. So, what are you going to do about this?"

"I'm going to talk to Do-Dirty."

"You need to do more than talk to his ass, you need to quit him before he gets our asses into some shit we can't get out of. Truth may be a sleazeball ass nigga, but the nigga ain't no hoe. He does get down, and like you, will kill something over his money. Don't let Do-Dirty start a war between the two of you." Baby Red's phone rings.

"Go on in there and get your nails done. I'm going to run these bags out to the car," he tells her while checking the caller ID on his phone and seeing the unknown incoming call. He answers the call while grabbing the bags out of her hand. "Billy Gunz, what's good baby?"

"What's going on lil dawg?" Baby Red broke down all the latest events including his mishap with Truth as he put the bags in the trunk of his Charger. "Yo bitch, Paris, is right though. If you can't control your cousin, you need to get rid of his ass before he causes you more problems than you need. War is bad for business in this game. A hustla needs his every focus on making money and not dealing with no unnecessary issues."

"I feel you, but I can handle Do-Dirty. I'm going to holla at him and put things back in shape with Truth."

"You better. Because it ain't just yo money in jeopardy."

"I know. And like I said, I got this."

"We'll see. What the stash look like?"

"I'm down to less than half a brick."

"Go make your confession around 4:30 tomorrow and you will have something soon. By then, have that situation with your cousin handled. I'm going to have you take that trip to Atlanta."

"You want me to meet with the plug?" Baby Red couldn't stop the smile that threatened to crease his face. That's exactly what he's been waiting for the opportunity to meet the plug. He figured with a little over two and a half months before Billy Gunz got out, he should have enough bread saved up to start buying his own bricks. That way he wouldn't have to pay middleman prices from Billy Gunz or anybody else.

"I want you to go pick up about twenty-five of them. You'll be following my white bitch, Missy, down there. She knows exactly what to do. Can you handle that?"

"You know you can count on me."

"Then I'll holla at you tomorrow." Billy Gunz disconnects the call.

After dropping Paris off at the crib to get ready for work, Baby Red parked on the corner of Richards and Locust and walked down the block to Eddie Cain's house. He knocked on the door and a tall malnourished crackhead with no teeth and a cane answered the door. "Baby Red what you know good my nigga?"

"What's going on Eddie Cain?"

"Ain't nothing change about Eddie Cain. I'm still smoking and ain't croaking. What brings you around here?"

"You saw my cousin Do-Dirty?"

"Oh, shit Do-Dirty in the back." Eddie steps aside letting Baby Red walk in. Three crackhead bitches sat on an old raggedy yellow and brown plaid couch taking turns taking hits from a glass pipe. The smell of dope and cheap tobacco lingered in the air. "He in the room in the back. The last door on the left at the end of the hall. I would escort you, nephew, but I got to take a hit before I hit the floor."

"Handle yo business, Eddie. I'll find my way." Baby Red makes a left out of the living room and walked down the hall. He reached the door where Do-Dirty was and opened it up. When he opened the door what he saw was an insult to his eyes. A Lesley Jones, "Planet of the Apes" looking crackhead bitch was bent over doggy style smoking a glass pipe while Do-Dirty was hitting her from the back. The smell of fishy pussy hung in the air. "What the fuck?"

"Oh shit, cuz. What you doing here?"

"I should be asking you that. Get dress and come holla at me."

"Alright give me a minute and I'll be there. You want some of this shit? This bitch got some good pussy."

"And some fire head too," she says, looking at Baby Red and showing her toothless smile.

"No thanks! Hurry up!" He closes the door and walks out of the house and sat on the porch.

Five minutes later, Do-Dirty comes walking out. "What the fuck is yo problem, Dirt?"

"What, the little dope head? I dope date sometimes, so what? I promise you, it comes out my pocket and not yours."

"I'm not talking about that. I'm talking about you making muscle moves without me. I never told you to set up shop. And on top of that, you take over one of Truth's spots."

"Man, fuck that pussy ass nigga. Cuz, I'll blow that nigga's top back. He don't scare me."

"It ain't about you being scared. It's all about respect. This ain't the West Side, cuz, shit is handled differently around these ways. Now, if you want to keep getting money with me, then go get all our shit out of there, and let's go." A crackhead comes walking up from the side of the house and onto the porch.

"Do-Dirty, can I get six for the fifty?" the crackhead says as he pulls a wrinkled fifty-dollar bill from his oil-stained jeans pocket.

"Come with it Boscoe," Do-Dirty says spitting five bags out his mouth and into his hand. The man hands him the fifty then takes his purchase and leaves. "This is a cash spot Baby Red! I'm going through almost a half-ounce of dope a night in this spot. These fiends love this shit we got. If we move around, all they going to do is hit us up anyway to come drop it off to them. Because they damn sho ain't going to be content with that mediocre dope Truth and his boys pushing." Baby Red knew what Do-Dirty was saying was the truth. But like Billy Gunz said, he got too much on the line to go to war right now. Weighing his option, he made the only decision he could make.

"We out of here. And if they call us, we serve them. Just not on his turf. That way we can dodge unnecessary problems and not lose a dollar in the midst."

"That's a lot of risks to be driving around with a lot of dope all day."

"You got a better suggestion?"

"Mookie's."

"Mookie's?"

"Dope fiend Mookie over there on Booth and North Avenue. That's off Truth's turf and it's still the East Side. Nobody got claims on Booth Street or on that end of North Avenue. We set up shop at Mookie's spot." Baby Red rubs his chin as he contemplated what Do-Dirty was suggesting.

"If we do this Dirt, you got to keep a cool head and a low profile. I don't need you getting all hothead with these niggas over here. And stay away from Truth's turf. I mean that Dirt. You fuck up, I'm cutting you off. Don't make me regret this."

"You got my word, cuz. I'll keep it cool and I'll stay clear of Truth's zone," Do-Dirty says as they shake hands.

Even though Do-Dirty gave Baby Red his word, Baby Red couldn't help but feel like he would soon regret his decision. In the meantime, he planned to keep an even closer eye on him. And to do that he decided to have Noodles and Pay Pay working alternating shifts with Do-Dirty at Mookie's spot, while their workers worked their spots on the West Side and Uptown. It was the only plan he had that put him at ease with keeping Do-Dirty around. A plan he hoped would work because if not, a lot could be lost from its outcome.

~ CHAPTER 5 ~

The ringing of his phone on the nightstand awaken him. Looking at the time, he saw that it was 4:27 AM. "Hello," he answers, wiping the sleep from his eyes.

"Did I wake you?"

"Hell yea, I had just fallen asleep two hours ago," he yearned as he spoke.

"Good, cause real hustlas don't sleep. You fall asleep in this game; you wake up to nightmares."

"Duly noted."

"I got what you dropped off yesterday at the confession booth."

"And it was all there, right? "

"As usual. Now, it's time for you to go make that pickup. Meet Missy at the Speedway gas station on Appleton Avenue in an hour."

"That's a white neighborhood. How am I supposed to pinpoint who she is?"

"Don't worry about that, she'll know who you are. Oh yea, and you might want to bring a suit."

"A suit?" After getting dressed, he grabbed his charcoal grey suit he had bought last year too for his aunt's wedding and headed out the door.

He pulls into the parking lot of the Speedway gas station. Even at 5:30 in the morning, the service station was busy. A lot of people coming in and out heading to work and other places. Baby Red tries to see if he could pinpoint which of the white bitches out there was Missy. It was harder to deduce than he thought it would be. Almost all of them looked like how Billy Gunz had described her in jail. They all looked professional with a couple of kids and a minivan.

His phone rings and the caller ID read unknown. He figured it had to be Billy Gunz.

"Yo, B. I'm here."

"Look across the street in the bank's parking lot," a female voice says on the other end. "You see the silver minivan with the Georgia license plates ready to pull out the parking lot?" He looks over and spots the minivan with its left turn signal activated.

"Yea, I see you."

"Stay two cars behind me at all times. I don't give out my number. If you need me, give your horn three quick taps and I'll hit your line. You got that?"

"Yea."

"Then let's go." Missy pulls out of the parking lot and Baby Red follows remembering to stay two cars behind her.

It was harder keeping up with her than he thought. Missy whipped that minivan like a NASCAR driver. After ten hours of traveling, he finally sees the 'Welcome to Atlanta' sign. Missy hits his line and tells him to check in at a different motel than her. He knew it was all about precaution. In case the police had an eye on him coming into town, they wouldn't see them as traveling together.

He checks in at a local motel close to downtown and waited for further instructions. While he waited, he adventured down the street to Krispy Kreme Doughnuts. The aroma of freshly made glazed doughnuts filled his nostrils and made his stomach growl as he walked through the door. He places an order for a dozen of fresh glazed doughnuts. Then from the corner of his eye he sees a black Dodge Challenger with limo tint just sitting outside. It was something about the car that gave him an uneasy feeling. It just set there as if whoever was in it was watching him. Without showing any signs to the driver that he noticed the car he gets his doughnuts and heads back to his motel room. Once inside the room he puts the doughnuts on the table and peeps out the blind to see if the car followed him. He scanned the parking lot and there was no sign of the car. He brushed it off and went to eat his doughnuts.

Unaware of the hypnotic taste of Krispy Kreme's doughnuts, he thought he could just eat two. Those two ended up with him eating the whole box and falling asleep.

***

"Yo, I don't need yo carpet munching ass to tell me how to handle my customers. If this nigga wants to smoke his shit here, he can smoke it here."

"All I'm saying, you stupid mothafucka, is if you going to let them smoke in here, then make their ass take that shit to the backroom! And clean this mothafucka up! It smells like musty balls and stale ass in this bitch."

"I'm surprised you even know what balls smell like."

"What, you mad I get mo' pussy than yo dope fiend humping ass? Yo ass ain't got to like me, and please know I'm not too fond of you either. These orders I'm giving you came from Baby Red himself. So, if you got a problem with anything that I just told you to do, then you take it up with him," Noodles says as she grabs the TV remote and sits on the couch.

"Yo, y'all take that shit to the back room," Do-Dirty reluctantly tells Mookie and the other smokers. "And when you done, Mookie, boil some bleach water and clean this place up." He plops down on the sofa chair in the living room and sparks a blunt to gathered his thoughts.

Even though the orders were coming from Baby Red, he still didn't need her delivering the message. It made him feel like a bitch was telling him what to do. Though it wouldn't have made it feel much better if it came from Pay Pay either.

To Do-Dirty, Pay Pay was a nigga with a bad attitude that didn't smile or talk much. He felt like Pay Pay was a nigga with a chip on his shoulders and Do-Dirty was looking for a reason to knock it off. He couldn't stand Pay Pay or Noodles. But most of all, he just hated the idea of having babysitters. This was his spot and his idea to take it over. He didn't want anybody looking over his shoulders telling him how to run shit. Do-Dirty loved feeling like the man in charge, but with Noodles and Pay Pay around, he felt more like a worker instead of a boss and Baby Red's partner.

When Baby Red recruited the three of them, he said they will all be his business partners just like Wee Wee was. But Do-Dirty was starting to feel like he was at the bottom of the food chain in that partnership. "I'll deal with this shit for about a month. Then if cuz can't see I'm fit to handle business on my own, well I guess some bridges will be burned and sacrifices will be made. I'll be damned if I don't get the respect I deserve," Do-Dirty said in his head as he watched Noodles play on her phone.

***

Hours later, Baby Red awakes from his nap and checks the time. 6:49 PM and still no call from Missy or Billy Gunz. After calling and checking on his business back home he hit the shower and got dressed. Might as well see the city while he waited.

After stopping off at the Underground Mall grabbing Paris a lil something and getting a quick bite to eat at Captain D's, he went to the place no out of town hustler could resist checking out. Magic City Gentlemen's Club.

The club was packed, and the dancers were way thicker than the one's back home. He went to the bar and ordered a

Cîroc and lime. Sipping his drink, his eyes scans the club and he noticed a few ballers was in attendance. He could tell they had long pockets by the ice on their wrist, neck, and fingers. Like Billy Gunz, some of them even had gold and diamonds all in their grill. "Damn, these Georgia boys eating," Baby Red says to himself as he watched one of the long pockets make it rain all hundreds on the bitch that was on stage.

The music stops and the girl on stage rises to her feet from the pool of blue face hundreds that she danced in. After collecting her money in a garbage bag, she exited the stage. Halsey's song, "Bad At Love" sang through the club speakers. A tall redhead White bitch with green eyes and an ass so fat it was unbelievable made her way to the stage. Baby Red was immediately mesmerized by her as she worked the pole with the energy of an Olympian and the grace of a swan. The dancer that had left the stage before her made her rounds around the club and stopped by Baby Red. "Would you like to tip me for my show?" she asked, but Baby Red couldn't take his eyes off the White girl on stage. He pulls a twenty out of his pocket and puts it in her G-string.

"Who is the bitch on stage?"

"That's what you like, huh?" Baby Red didn't reply, he just kept his eyes on the stage. "That's Classy, she's cool people. If you want to rap with her, I suggest you ask her for a lap dance. Because time is money with her and it's a lot of niggas in this club that's ready to spend them both with her."

"I'm good, white girls ain't my type." She laughs.

"Classy is everybody's type," she says before walking off. Baby Red continues enjoying the show. One man puts a ten-dollar bill in his mouth and Classy pushes his head between her big 38DD breast and shakes them on his face. Then she squeezes her breast together to grab the ten out of his mouth.

After a couple of songs, Classy gathers her sea of bills and clears the stage. She makes her rounds and when she gets to Baby Red, she says, "I feel cheated by you."

"What you mean, lil baby?" he replies with a confused look.

"You never took your eyes off me when I was on stage, so I know you liked my show. But you never came up and tipped me," she says with her arms folded across her chest. He digs in his pockets and pulled out a hundred.

"I was waiting for you to come give me a lap dance." She smiles and takes the hundred then leads him to the lap dance booth.

He admires her tan skin and firm body. He had never seen a white girl with an ass so fat and couldn't help but wonder if it was real. As if reading his mind, she puts his hands on it and says, "Oh, it's real, if that's what you're wondering." It was firm with a nice jiggle to it.

"It most certainly feels real. Damn, I can't lie they don't make white girls like you back home." She mounts on top of him and grinds on him moving her body to the beat of the music.

"And where's home?"

"Milwaukee, Wisconsin. You ever been?"

"The city of beer and state of cheese. No, I have never been."

"What a shame."

"What brings you to Georgia?"

"Business."

"What kind of business?"

"The kind that puts food on the table, Ferragamo on my back, and a woman like you in my lap."

"How long you're in town for?"

"Just until I'm done taking care of business."

"Are you always this indirect with your answers?"

"Do you always ask your spenders so many questions?"

"Just the chosen few I wish to get to know," she says with her face so close that their noses touch.

"If you are trying to get to know me, then how about we grab a bite to eat when you get off and chop it up?"

"I'll think about it." She turns around reverse cowgirl style leaning back on him with her arm around the back of his neck as she grinds on him. The vanilla fragrance she wore he found intoxicating and at the same time stimulating as his manhood begin to take full salute. She felt his bulge and grind harder.

"Well you better think quick because when this lap dance is over, I'm going to polish off another drink then I'm out."

"What's the rush?"

"Clubs ain't really my thing. I just came out for a quick drink and see what the ass look like in Atlanta. Now, my mission is accomplished." The song plays out and the lap dance comes to an end.

"In that case, meet me at closing and I'll show you what more Atlanta has to offer," she says, planting a kiss on his cheeks before walking away.

After sharing a meal and getting to know each other, a connection was made. She told him about her life and growing up in Georgia while he told her all about having a wifey and his life back home. They spent two hours conversing before going back to his motel room.

Baby Red never cheated on Paris before and didn't know what it was about this White bitch that had him ready to cross lines he never dared to cross before. Temptation was a mothafucka and they both were happy to give into its pleasures as his lips caress hers and their tongues wrestled in each other's mouths for dominance. The burning desire of their lust had them coming out of their clothes as fast as they could remove

47

them. She pushes him onto the bed and straddles him, then slides him inside of her. And as his member penetrates her tight velvet fortress, her eyes roll in the back of her head and he bites his lower lip. She releases a long sexy moan that made him throb inside of her. They spent the next couple hours passionately exploring each other's bodies until they reached a mutual climax that forced them into a state of weakness.

The sound of his phone ringing awakens him. "Hello."

"Meet me at this address in an hour. Put on your suit and don't be late." Baby Red jots down the address that Missy gave him and then checks the time, 8:03 AM. He looks over at the bed and sees Classy still asleep. He gets dressed then wakes her.

"Baby girl, I got to roll, but you can stay here and sleep. Checkout ain't 'til noon." She stretched and yawns.

"Will I see you again?"

"I don't see why not. You got my number, call me," he says with a hug and a kiss. He could've gone for another round in the sheets with her before leaving, but business always comes first. He opens the door to leave, and as he steps out of the room, he sees that familiar-looking black Charger start up and pull out the parking lot of the motel. "Is that the police or is it some nigga following me? Stop tripping, Baby Red. It's Sunday, maybe that's some nigga from around here who caught him a lil bitch at the club last night and brought her to the telly," he thought to himself as he got in his car to leave.

~ CHAPTER 6 ~

The address Missy gave him lead him to a huge church on the West Side of Atlanta. His phone rings as he pulls in the Walmart size parking lot. Automatically knowing it was Missy he answers the phone. "I think I got the wrong address."

"No, you are in the right place. I'm parked in section C towards the middle of the parking lot. Pull into the parking space right beside me." He turns down section C and spots Missy. She was wiping one of the kid's face off while the other played in the empty parking spot next to their van. He taps his horn and she commands the boy to her side. After claiming the parking spot, he gets out. Without even turning around she says, "Just go in there and grab a seat on the far-left side close to the back of the church and keep an eye on me." Baby Red had many questions, but he thought best to save them for later.

He went inside the church whose lobby looked like the lobby of a museum. It had a gift shop where they sold Bibles and just about anything with Jesus on it. Four ATMs sat in the lobby giving people no excuse for not having an offering to put in the collection plate. Inside the church area, was a camera crew and a stage fit for Reverend Take-Yo-Dolla to put on his show.

Baby Red believed in God, but not in church. To him, church was one of the biggest scams legally ran on people.

He takes a seat on the far-left side of the church three pews from the back. Shortly after, Missy comes in with a large diaper bag and her two kids. She takes a seat in the row to the right of him one pew up. After the choir sang their praises, the Televangelist Reverend Kevin Dollar started preaching his sermon. "Today church, I will be reading from the First Epistle of Paul. That's Paul Chapter 6:9 and 10. And it reads as follows:

'But they that will be rich fall into temptation and a snare, and into many foolish and hurtful lusts, which drown men in destruction and prediction...' Then verse 10 reads: 'For the love of money is the root of all evil: which while some coveted after, they have erred from the faith, and pierced themselves through with many sorrows...'

Now church, I was a man of the world before I took Jesus Christ as my savior." The church begins to ad-lib him with shouts of amen as he preached. "I was a hustla, a pimp, a drug addict, a thief, and gang banger. I know the temptations of the almighty dollar. And I know the high you get from the fame, materialistic gain, and fallacious love that comes with it. The feeling of being on top of the world it gives you. But I also know the troubles that come with it. The penitentiary, the grave amongst many other struggles. It's the devil's snare. And in the end, most lose more than they ever gained when they play the devil's game." The next thing he knew, Baby Red could've sworn the Reverend was looking dead at him when he spoke his next words. "Just remember, church, what was in James Chapter 1:12: 'Blessed is the man that endureth temptation. For when he is tried, he shall receive the crown of life, which the Lord had promised to them that love him'."

Church begins to let out and as Missy got up a Mexican woman holding a toddler approached her. They sat down their matching diaper bags and gave each other a hug. The two women talked a few minutes then the Mexican woman picked up Missy's bag and left. Missy picked up the woman's bag and walked out. A few seconds later Baby Red made tracks behind her. She makes a pit stop in the bathroom. Her oldest kid stood outside of the restroom door swinging the diaper bag. Baby Red takes a few sips of water from the bubbler nearby. The little boy was next to him digging in the diaper bag. Baby Red couldn't help but wonder what was in the diaper bag the

Mexican woman left Missy carrying. It was a big bag, but it was no way it was holding twenty-five kilos of dope. He peeked over and seen it was filled with nothing more than wet wipes, candy, a baby bottle, and some pull-ups. The little boy snuck a few pieces of candy out of the bag and put it in his pocket.

They get to the parking lot and she gives him his next orders. "Okay, it's the same rules as it was coming here. Stay two cars behind and if you need me, give the horn three quick taps," she tells him as she buckles the kids in.

"We heading back already? What about picking up the shit?"

"Ooh mommy, that man said a bad word," the oldest kids says.

"And at church," the youngest one adds in.

"Language!" Missy tells Baby Red.

"My bad. The stuff?"

"Everything's taken care of. We just have to get back safe and sound. If I get pulled over, take the next exit and keep looping around until they let me go. If they bring a dog and search the van, your job is to make sure me, these kids, and that van get away by all means. You got that?"

"Yea, I got you."

"Then let's not waste any more time and hit this highway," she says, sliding the minivan's side door shut and hopping into the driver's seat.

Missy seemed to have done this many times before. She knew what she was doing and had that take-charge attitude to go along with it. She looked like a Wall Street businesswoman and carried herself like an owner of a Fortune 500 company, but she was no doubt a thoroughbred hustler. Baby Red admired Billy Gunz for having such a winner like that on his team. Billy Gunz's whole operation was run with paranoia.

But Baby Red couldn't front; the way he moved in secrecy and silence was smooth. At the same time, he couldn't help but feel a bit disappointed he didn't meet the plug like he thought he was.

Making it back to the Mil with no issues, Missy and Baby Red parted ways on the highway without stopping. She told him his package would be dropped off to him as usual. He went to the South Side and check the money at Wee Wee's spot.

Since Paris had already picked up the bread last night and dropped him off some more work, it wasn't much to collect. He sat on the couch blowing a blunt with Wee Wee and telling him all about Classy and his trip to Magic City.

"You? My nigga, you? Mr. Give Me Ebony Over Ivory Any Day shook sheets with a White bitch? Nahhh!"

"I'm serious, my nigga. I'm just as shocked as you. It was just something about this bitch."

"Probably all that ass you said she had," Wee Wee says while pouring a double shot of Amsterdam in his glass.

"That mothafucka was fat! But it was something else. Some deeper connection than that."

"Yea, but you better be careful not to let shit get too deep. You know Paris' ass is crazy as a mothafucka. She doesn't like to share, and she won't play fair," he says, passing Baby Red the blunt and taking a sip of his drink. Wee Wee being Paris's cousin was all too familiar with her jealous ways.

"I mean, I'm digging lil mama. She's a nice knock for the boots and she gives me good vibes. But it ain't like I'm falling in love with the bitch or anything. I mean, I just met her and we just going to have good times whenever I'm in town."

"So, she going to be your Georgia girl, huh? Just something to keep you company when you in town."

"Something like that." A crackhead comes up from the basement.

"Wee Wee, you got some Chore Boy?" she says scratching under her bra strap.

"Yup, fifty cents a brillo pad," he tells her, pulling a box off the shelf and pulling one out. She dug into her dinghy pants pocket and pulled out the change. She gets her purchase and runs back downstairs. "Do you, my nigga. Just don't let my crazy ass cousin find out or you might wake up without your penis."

With Paris already had done made the pickups and drop-offs last night, there was no need to stop at any of the other spots, so he headed home to count his money and kick in a little quality time with her.

"Oh my God, baby! I love them!" Paris says excitedly as she tries on the Red Bottom shoes that he copped for her at the Underground Mall along with a Gucci dress.

"I want you to wear all that next month for me."

"Why next month?"

"I'm taking you and the rest of the team out to Club Swag. I hear Plies and Yo Gotti will be performing. And I know how much you love Yo Gotti."

"And you know it!" she says with much excitement in her voice. She climbs on top of him. "You know I missed you while you were gone, right?"

"How much did you miss me?"

"This much." She starts kissing wet trails down his neck and chest. But before things could get too heated, his phone rings, followed by a knock at the door. "Something always got to kill the mood these days," she says, getting up to answer the door. Baby Red answers the phone.

"Yea."

"Missy tells me you did good today."

"I didn't know I was going just to play the sacrificial lamb if things went wrong. It would've been nice to been given the heads up on that."

"You should know by now how I move, Baby Red. Real hustlas like killas move in silence, tell nobody shit. You told me you were a hustla and wanted to level up in this game. You said you dreamed of being the man and you're willing to get there by any means necessary. I'm just giving you the opportunity you have never been given to make those dreams come true. So why question my methods of getting you there?" Paris closes the door and walks in dragging a toddler's bed mattress and letting it fall to the living room floor as she slumps down on the couch next to Baby Red.

"It's just you so paranoid and secretive about everything it makes it hard for me to believe you really want to help me get there. I mean, instead of meeting the plug, you had me go all the way down to Georgia to attend Sunday services and be a sacrifice if things went wrong. I just don't see how that was supposed to put me on the road to being the man."

"If you can't see the things that I'm teaching you along the way, then I think I picked the wrong student to give the secrets of the game. If a hustla ain't paranoid, then he ain't really moving shit. And that lets me know you ain't ready to be the man. A mothafucka gives you the keys to the kingdom right now and you would be dead or rotting in the joint in less than a few months. You want to meet the plug, that's every po' hustla's dream. That takes baby steps to get there. In the meantime, keep yo eyes open at all times and know everything I do comes with a logical reason." Billy Gunz disconnects the call. Paris hands him a knife. Baby Red puts the phone away and gets on the floor and begins cutting open the mattress. He retrieves twelve keys out of the mattress then he and Paris begin busting them down.

After busting the bricks down and giving Paris her sexual attention, they lay in bed asleep. His phone rings. He looks at the caller ID and sees it was Classy. He slipped out of bed, careful not to awake Paris, and walked outside to take the call. "What's up beautiful?"

"Hey, you," she says with loud music playing in the background.

"You at work?"

"Yea. I was thinking about you and had to give you a call."

"Missing me already?"

"I guess you can say that." A smile creases his face. He sparks the blunt he grabbed off the kitchen table on the way out. "When am I going to see you again?"

"The way business be going here I'm sure I'll be back down there real soon," he says, sucking in a cloud of weed smoke.

"I hope so because I can't wait to show you more of Atlanta and more of me," she says seductively. "Well baby, I've got to go. I'm next up on stage. Talk to you later, muah," she says, giving him a kiss through the phone and hanging up. With a huge smile on his face, he turns around to go back inside and his heart could've jumped out his chest when he saw Paris standing in the doorway.

"Damn, you scared me. What the hell you doing standing there?"

"No, what the hell you doing out here? And who the hell you on the phone with this time of night that got you smiling like a trick in a cunt factory?" she says with her hand on her hip and her New York-style Cuban accent pouring out thick.

"That was Do-Dirty, baby. We were just kicking the shit. I didn't want to wake you with my loud as mouth, so I came out here," he says, walking up on her.

"That better be the reason," she says with her arms crossed and a mug on her face.

"It was the only reason, baby. You were sleeping too good. You had drool coming down the side of yo mouth. Look, you got a slob stain right there." He points to a spot on her cheeks. She smacks his hand away.

"Shut up and get in this house." He kisses her on the cheek and walks passed her into the house. Paris let it go, but she knew Baby Red wasn't telling her the truth about that phone call. And now with her suspicion raised, she planned to keep her eyes open. I guess you could say the guilt of taking Baby Red from Tokyo makes her worry if he would leave her for another woman. Her mother always told her what goes around comes around and karma is the bitch that brings it.

~ CHAPTER 7 ~

The sun shined down hard bringing its sweltering heat with it. Women walked around in short shorts and bikini tops. It got so hot someone in the neighborhood opened the cap on the fire hydride and all the kids in the neighborhood played in its flowing waters. Do-Dirty and Pay Pay sat on the porch drinking beers watching life on the block while Noodles sat inside keeping an eye on the smokers in the house. A loud noise comes from inside the house. The sound of arguing and glass breaking. "Nigga you stole that rock out my pipe!" Someone yelled from inside.

"Don't you think you should go and there and take care of that?" Pay Pay tells Do-Dirty. Do-Dirty took a swig of his beer and didn't budge.

"Let the dike take care of it. She wants to be a man so bad let her ass take care of it." The fighting inside continued and Noodles could be heard trying to break it up.

"But this is yo spot and shit like that will bring heat over here."

"If this was my spot, then y'all ass wouldn't be here. So, since you and that clit nibbler want to play my mama and daddy, go handle yo business." A man pulls up on a ten-speed bike sweating hard. "Besides, I got a customer to attend to," he says taking another swig of his beer and gets up to serve the man. Pay Pay, irritated with him and his lack of responsibility, mugs him and shakes his head to keep from beating his ass, goes in and handle it himself. "Bitch ass nigga," Do-Dirty whispers to himself. "What you need, Rick James? And why yo ass sweating so damn much?" Rick James pulls out a crumpled-up McDonald's napkin and wipes the sweat from his forehead. Rick James spoke like a pimp and dressed like it was the 80's.

"Man, it's hotter than ass on the devil's hookers' baby! And I had to peddle my ass all the way over here from First and Keefe Street. Give me get ten of them and let me get a blessing, baby." He pulls out a fold of wrinkled bills from his pocket. Do-Dirty grabs his dope bag out the bushes and gives him twelve.

"Here's two extra on me."

"Thanks, Do-Dirty! You know I like blessings, baby. Man, I sho wish you open up shop down there. You do that and yo ass would be the man! I know all the smokers over there! And I got my own crib you can setup shop in."

"First and Keefe? That sounds tempting, but that's Truth territory."

"Man, fuck him! You hear me? That nigga's dope ain't shit. This shit you hustling got us walking around her like zombies', baby. I mean, look at me. I'm forty-seven years old and I'm out here peddling a bicycle jack! All the way over here just to come get this shit from you when Truth got four spots along the way. You hear me? I'm telling you that you can have this shit on lock you come over there."

"I tell you what, let me think about it. You got a phone?"

"Hell yea. Obama made sure we all had phones baby," Rick James says, pulling out his cell phone. Do-Dirty takes his number down. Rick James puts the rocks under his tongue and jumps on his bike and leaves. Pay Pay and Noodles come out tossing two crackheads out the house.

"What, you couldn't help?" Noodles ask him with a mug on her face.

"Don't y'all supposed to keep me out of trouble? If you were expecting me to handle that then what the hell y'all here for?" He swallows the last gulp of his beer, burps, then tosses the empty beer bottle in the bushes and hops off the porch. "Well mom, pops, I'll be back. I'm going to get more beer.

Don't worry, I promise not to get in any trouble along the way. Okay?"

***

Baby Red finds himself lying in bed sweating profusely and trying to catch his breath after putting in work nailing Classy from the back for the last hour. Classy had flown to Madison, Wisconsin to work a week at The Doll House Gentlemen's Club as a special guest dancer. It was good enough excuse for her to come down and spend more time with Baby Red and he was more than happy to see her again so soon. "Get that pretty pink ass of yours up and go roll me a blunt." He smacks her on her naked ass, and she hops out of bed. She grabs the blunts off the hotel dresser right next to the TV.

"I see the blunts, but where's the weed?"

"Look in my pants pocket." She digs in his pocket and grabs the half-ounce of Kush and an 8-ball of coke falls out with it. She picks it up and shows it to him.

"Baby Red, is this coke?"

"Yea."

"I want some."

"You get down?"

"Just here and there to have a good time."

"Then bust that bitch open and let's have a good time." She pulls out her makeup mirror and poured some powder on it and started forming it into four thin lines.

"You got a straw?" He shakes his head no. She looks around the room for something to use and spots an ink pen on the nightstand. Removing the ink insert and cap on the other end, she had the straw she needed. She blew one line and felt the kick of it. "Whoa! That shit is -" She pauses, feeling her nose starting to run she sniffs hard twice before continuing. "That shit is heaven."

"I would think you should be used to coke that potent. I mean it did come from your city." She blows another line.

"No, you may have met with your plug there, but that didn't come from Georgia. I would know, I know all the big dealers in Georgia because they all come to the club. I've tried all their shit and none of them have ever had anything this potent," she says, passing him the mirror and pen.

"Maybe it did come from there and they just stepped on their shit too much." He puts the pen to his nose and clears the two lines and passes her back the mirror.

"Maybe, but I doubt it. Because like all real hustlers, they pride themselves on having better dope than the next hustler. If you were to bring some of this down there and with me working in the club where all the ballers be and coke head dancers, and you see how much money they get, baby you'll be rich in no time. I know you got your business here, but why eat off just one table when you have two at your disposal? You should really think about that. Hell, you would sell out so fast your plug probably wouldn't even be able to keep up with you," she says, rolling a blunt.

The wheels in Baby Red's mind begin turning. *If this shit booms down there like she says it would then I can really take over the game. I could have Classy like Billy Gunz have Missy. Make that bitch hit the highway with the bricks and I follow her there. She's right. Why eat off one table when I got two?* he thinks to himself.

"I tell you what, if shit is popping like you said it is out there, we can definitely start flooding the city down there with this shit." He grabs the blunt from her and takes a pull. He holds it in a moment then blows it out his nose. "But before I start bringing some major work those ways, I'm going to send a couple of people from my team out there with a lil work and see how that shit goes." She puts together another round of lines and blows two.

"It sounds like a good plan to me, daddy," she says, passing him the mirror in exchange for the blunt. He vacuums up the two thin lines and lays back in the bed. He couldn't help but think of all the money he would be making if all this shit was to pan out. He would run out of work so fast and so often Billy Gunz wouldn't have any choice but to introduce him to the plug. And once he got the plug it was no doubt in his mind, he was going to take over the game.

***

"Do-Dirty! Come on in. Welcome to Ricky Enterprises, baby!" Rick James says, inviting Do-Dirty in and giving him a tour of his small two-bedroom apartment. Rick James introduced him to two of his White crack buddies that work at the factory with him. They were sitting around smoking some dope they had got from one of Truth's spots when Do-Dirty approached them.

"How about y'all show a lil mercy to your lungs and stop smoking that bullshit. Take a hit of this," Do-Dirty tells them as he hands them each a dime sack.

"My man came with samples. Fat sacks too. I like you already," Jerry, one of the smokers, say. After finishing their hits, Doug, the other smoker, begins setting up the pipe so they could try what Do-Dirty gave them. He sparked his lighter and the flame shot up four inches in the air. A crackling sound was made as he sucked in the smoke from the pipe. After he took a hit, he held it in and passed the pipe to Jerry. He blew the smoke out and sat there staring out into space. Jerry took his hit and his eyes got big, he started sweating and couldn't stop fidgeting. "Holy Shit! That's a good high. Let me by an 8-ball of that."

"He charges two hundred for his 8-balls, Jerrys" Rick James says winking his eye at Do-Dirty. He knew Rick James was on a hustle to put a little extra in both of their pockets because Rick James knew he only charged a hundred for his 8-balls.

"I'll pay that."

"So that means a quarter is four hundred?" Doug says, slowly coming back to earth.

"Yup, but y'all know y'all still got to bless Rick James with a piece for making these deals and giving you a safe place to get high. Rick James likes his blessings, baby."

"That's cool, I'll take a quarter." Do-Dirty collects their money and walks into the other room and starts putting together their purchase. Rick James joins him.

"I told you it's money over here. And that ain't even the customers I have over this way. Them just some honkies that I work with. Just wait 'til tonight."

"Why tonight?"

"Because the fiends come out at night, fiends come out at night," he begins to sing those words and dance.

"It's the freaks come out at night."

"Yea, well around here is like the *Night of the Living Dead*. All the zombies come out at night searching for their high. You'll see."

"That I will." Do-Dirty got ready to leave out the room, but Rick James stopped him.

"Whoa Whoa! Slow down, brother. Rick James needs his blessing, baby." Do-Dirty cuts him off a sixteenth. "That's what I'm talking about. Hustlas hustles go up and Rick James's blessings come down, baby." He kisses the sack. "Time for me to get high."

It was only 11:30 and Do-Dirty had already sold a who ounce worth of dope at Rick James's spot. He headed back to Mookie's to re-up.

"Here this nigga go now y'all!" Noodles yells from the porch into the house. "Where the fuck you been?"

"Minding my mothafuck'n business and not yours."

"How is that when your business is here? Or is you out making business elsewhere?"

"Man, watch out. I don't answer to bitches, they answer to me," he says, pushing past her and taking a seat in one of the chairs on the porch.

"Yea, but you going to answer to me," Baby Red says coming out of the house. "Where you been, Dirt? It's been a house full of mothafuckas trying to get high and you ain't nowhere to be found."

"I left they ass with my sack. They should've got that shit off."

"Bitch ass nigga I don't work for you." Pay Pay tells him from the other end of the porch. Do-Dirty gets up in gets in Pay Pay's face.

"You better watch that bitch word, nigga, before you be swallowing some teeth with it." Pay Pay, standing at 5'11" and 200 pounds of solid muscles, takes off his shirt and faces off with Do-Dirty who stood 6'2" and 170 pounds.

"I wish yo soft ass would. I've been waiting for the opportunity to whoop yo ass." Baby Red steps in the middle of them breaking it up before it even got started.

"Fuck that Baby Red! Let Pay Pay whoop that nigga's ass. Lord knows that boy needs it."

"Shut the fuck up, Wee Wee. We all know you can't fight."

"But I sho know how to shoot me a nigga," Wee Wee tells Do-Dirty while waving his gun for him to see.

"Everybody chill the fuck out!" Pay Pay and Do-Dirty back away from each other without taking their eyes off one another. Baby Red turns his attention back to Do-Dirty. "As I was saying, mothafuckas hustled your sack off and theirs. So, where you been?"

"Look, you got me cooped up in here with these two mothafuckas who watching everything I do like I'm a kid or something. I had gone by one of my bitch's houses to blow off a little steam. Is that okay with you, pops?"

"If you wasn't such a liability Dirt, I wouldn't have to have them here with you all the time."

"If you feel like I'm such a liability, then why even have me as your partner? And speaking of partners, when you going to start treating me like one and not like your worker? All I'm asking is that you let me run shit over here the way I want to and without them. I'll follow your little guidelines, just let me do me. Just like you let them do them at their spots. That way they can go back to focusing on their spots and I can focus on mine without all the added stress."

"The idiot makes sense in a way. Noodles and I can't keep coming over here, Baby Red, babysitting this nigga. We got our own spots to look after and then with this trip to Georgia that you want us to take. Either cut him loose or roll with his plan."

"Georgia? What they going to Georgia for?"

"They going down there to see how business flow in case we setup shop down them ways too. But as far as letting you do you..." Baby Red fought hard not to let the words fall out of his mouth. But weighing all his options he sees he can't cut him loose because he promised his aunt before she died, he would always take care of her only child and that promise he swore he would never break. As much as he hated to do so, he dropped the leash around Do-Dirty's neck. "Do you."

~ CHAPTER 8 ~

"Touchdown," Pay Pay says on the other end of the phone.

"Good. Remember only fuck with the niggas Classy sends y'all way. She's in good with the bouncers in the club, so they'll make sure y'all get in with y'all heats and turn their backs on any deals y'all make. Just make sure you hit their hand at the end of the night."

"Consider it done. Everything good out them ways?"

"Yea me and Wee Wee been keeping an eye on all the spots and Do-Dirty haven't been stirring up any trouble that I know of. So, yea, shit is straight."

"That's what's up. I'm going to let you go though, me and Noodles finna head to the club."

"Alright, peace."

"Peace." Baby Red sent Pay Pay and Noodles down to Georgia with nine ounces to test the waters. He had Classy dress up in business attire, wrap her hair in a bun and even put on a pair of prescription glasses making her look more like a sexy lawyer then a stripper. He had her rent a minivan and they loaded it up with the dope and guns. Them making it down there safely with all the work was just half of the mission. Now they have to get it all off while dodging any issues that may arise along the way.

Classy met Pay Pay and Noodles at the door of the club and the bouncers let them walk right in without getting a pat-down. "I reserved that table over there in the corner for the two of you. It's a low-key spot where you can chill and make your transactions. The girls here use that spot to give their customers special attention if you know what I mean. When somebody wants something, I'll walk them over to you. Until then, just enjoy yourselves." Classy says before leaving them to attend to the people in the club that came to spend on her.

"I can definitely see why Baby Red stepped out on Paris for her. Look at the ass on her, shaped just like a Georgia peach. That must be the forbidden fruit Eve made Adam eat," Pay Pay says, causing Noodles to laugh.

"You know that's the most words I ever heard you speak that wasn't about money. I'm starting to think you're actually human after all."

"It's not that I don't have anything other than money to talk about. It's I don't talk to people I don't know or don't like about anything other than money. Because the way I see it, the only thing they could do for me is break bread or move the fuck around."

"Yo, I'm feeling yo philosophy on that. I mean, why waste time talking to a mothafucka who ain't on what you on, right? Either talk bread or be dead to me."

"My point exactly." Two beers are brought over to their table from one of the dancers.

"Classy asked me to bring these to y'all."

"Good looking out," Noodles tells her and puts a five-dollar bill in her G-string.

"No problem. My name is Lexus and just let me know if yo sexy ass needs anything else."

"Will do baby," Noodles tells her while checking out her cheeks as she walks off with a seductive smile on her face. Noodles takes a swig out of the bottle Budweiser. "Yo, I'm getting some of that before we go back home."

"I don't blame you. Lil mama got some nice cheeks on her. It's like damn is all the bitches down these ways just as thick as a Snickers. I'm loving this shit!"

"Amen!" They toast their bottles.

"I take it that I must be one of the few people you like?"

"We conversing about things besides money ain't we? You cool. I fucks with you, Noodles. You're not like the rest of them niggas. You got a good head on your shoulders and I know if shit was to ever hit the fan, you would have my back. That's why when Baby Red suggested I bring Wee Wee instead of you, I told him it was either you or I wasn't going."

"It's obvious why you didn't want to bring Do-Dirty. But why not Wee Wee?"

"Wee Wee alright, but he still has childish ways that distract him from being on point at times. And in this game where your life is on the line at all times, I can't trust him to be the nigga watching my back." Hearing that Noodles couldn't help but feel how special she must be to Pay Pay. She never knew he felt that way and thought so deep about shit. She gained a newfound respect for him. Classy comes over to the table.

"I just gave Big Country a sample and he went to the bathroom to try it out. If he likes that shit, which I know he will, he'll buy a whole ounce of it off top. I know Baby Red sales his zips for a grand. But don't be afraid to tax these fuckers twelve hundred. Trust me, they'll pay it. Here he comes now." A tall heavyset man who looked like a dark-skinned E-40 comes walking out the bathroom. He comes to the table sniffing and pinching the tip of his nose.

"Classy, these yo people with that there?"

"Yea, this Pay Pay and Noodles. Whatever you need, sweety, they got you." He takes a seat in front of them at the table and pulls out a bankroll.

"What you want for an ounce of that there?"

"Twelve-hundred dollars," Noodles tells him.

"Well, give me four of them mothafuckas. And make sure them hoes don't lose weight before they get to me," Big Country says, passing them the money under the table. Noodles slips a hand under her sports bra and pulls out the four ounces and hands it to him under the table. Big country feels the bags in his hands for a moment. "Yea, it's all there. I'll be to see y'all again shortly," he says, tucking the zips into his draws and stashing them under his nuts before walking off.

"Damn, we down to five zips already."

"I told Baby Red nine wouldn't be enough. That shit is going to be gone in the next couple of days," Classy says, leaving to round up some more customers.

***

"Remember what I told you. Never tell a mothafucka you hustling for me. In fact, never mention my name. Here take this." Do-Dirty hands him a 9mm. "You know how to use it?" The lil nigga smacks his lips.

"Man, yea, I know how to use it."

"Then if a nigga charge you up about hustling over here, bust their ass on site. You hear me?"

"I hear that. I got no problem with putting a nigga in the dirt over this paper, Do-Dirty."

"Yea, I see you got heart, lil nigga. I like that in you. Now let's get this cheese."

Business has been popping for Do-Dirty in both his spots. His only problem was when he left from one spot to the other, he was missing out on money. So, he hired Tank, a fourteen-year-old lil nigga from his old block to come work Rick James' spot while he worked Mookie's. That way Baby Red and no one else would be the wiser to him having another spot, and on Truth's turf.

Do-Dirty is just one of those shiesty niggas who don't give a fuck who he has to use or fuck over to get what he wants, so using young naive ass Tank was no moral downfall for him. He was going to the top of the food chain by all means necessary.

Meanwhile, Rick James' own sense of greed started to kick in. Truth's spots near him had been doing so bad since Do-Dirty setup shop there, they had to start selling their twenties as dimes just to keep people coming. Rick James found this out and immediately started capitalizing off of it. He would go and buy a few bags then bust them down and mixing them with some of Do-Dirty's work without him knowing. It was easy because Tank was lazy. He played video games all day and would let Rick James serve everybody who came when he was deep off into his games, which was all the time. In the end, Rick James would end up more than doubling his blessings.

"Ticky! I need a blessing, baby," Rick James says, pulling up to Ticky's spot. Ticky is Truth's, right-hand man. They called him Ticky because he had a short fuse and was like a walking time bomb ready to explode at any time on anybody.

Rick James hops off the bike combing his jerry curl to the back. "I came to spend sixty with you this time. Don't give me no bullshit now. Get me one of those sixteenths, baby, with a blessing on top." Rick James hands him the money.

"Come in the house." He follows Ticky inside the house. Rick James could see from the front door past the living room and dining room into the kitchen. Ticky's bitch stood in there with a chopper strapped around her neck cooking fish and spaghetti. Entering into the front room, a pit bull charges at his leg growling and showing its teeth but is yanked back by its chain that was locked to a metal ring drilled into the wall. Rick James jumps back.

"Watch your step, they ain't too fond of company." Two more pit bulls were chained to opposite walls growling and other dogs could be heard barking in the back. Rick James eases pass and follows Ticky into the dining room that sat between the kitchen and living room. Ticky pulls out a scale and weighs out a sixteenth and throws in a little extra for him.

"Rick James, you wouldn't know nothing about why business has been so slow lately, would you?"

"I have no clue."

"I know all these mothafuckas ain't checked into rehab or went cold turkey. You ain't heard nothing about any fools around here hustling on Truth's turf, have you?"

"Hell nah! You think if I did, I would be peddling over here to come buy from yo ass with these crazy-ass dogs?" Ticky hands him the dope.

"You hear something, let me know and I'll bless you real good."

"Yes indeed. You know I love blessings, baby."

***

Pay Pay and Noodles make it back to the motel room Baby Red had Classy get for them in a hype's name in case something went down their names wouldn't be attached to the room. The room wasn't anything fancy. Just two nightstands, a dresser that a 32" television sat on, and two queen size beds. It was three in the morning and they were down to only three ounces already. They were too geeked to go to sleep. Pay Pay sat on his bed counting the money. Noodles pulls out a bottle of Seagram's gin she bought earlier that day. She twists off the cap and takes a drink then passes it to Pay Pay. "Nah I'm good." He continues counting money.

"Come on Pay Pay, I know you ain't finna make me drink alone. I hate drinking alone."

"Gin makes you sin."

"So, let's dance with the devil, choirboy."

"If I drink with you will you let me be for the rest of the morning?"

"Only if you finish the whole bottle with me. If not, I'll make sure you don't get no sleep tonight. I'm so lit right now I will talk to you from sunup 'til sundown. And you know I will. So, what's it going to be Pay Pay?" She waves the bottle in his face. He snatches the bottle out her hand and takes a heavy gulp of it. He grunts as he feels the burn of it in his chest.

Thirty minutes later, the bottle sat empty on the nightstand while Noodles and Pay Pay sat next to each other on the bed talking. Both of them drunk and slurring their words as they talked. "I want to ask you something and be honest with me. Don't lie! I hate liars, so keep it real."

"Alright, I'm going to keep it 100 with you."

"Did you," she says pointing to him then herself. "mean what you said about me back there at the club tonight, last night or whenever the hell it was?"

"What did I say?"

"You said you liked me, and I was special to you."

"I didn't say that. I said that?"

"Well, you said something like that. Is that what you feel about me? Remember to keep it one-hundred."

"I'ma keep it one-hundred with you. I like you."

"I like you too."

"No, you don't."

"Yes, I do."

"Prove it." She gives him a quick peck on the lips.

"See."

"Nah."

"What you mean, nah?"

"You like me like that, but I like you like this." He grabs her face, presses his lips against hers, and lets his tongue massage its way into her mouth. She pushes him back. "You know

what? My bad, I probably shouldn't have gone there with you."
Noodles stands up and starts coming out of her clothes. Pay
Pay couldn't believe the body she hid under all the baggy
clothes she wore. She got on top of him and buried her tongue
in his mouth as he started snatching off his own clothes. Drunk
off gin and lust, they rumbled in the bed until the sun gave full
shine over the horizon.

~ CHAPTER 9 ~

Ticky stood in the backyard with a water hose bathing his prized fighter. A short and stocky dark brindle pit bull with cropped ears named Ms. Bitch. She just won another fight bringing her record up to thirty-seven wins, twenty-three of them kills and zero losses. Ticky had much pride in her. "Good girl, Ms. Bitch, good girl," he tells her as he cleans the blood from the other dog off her. Dee Dee, Ticky's girl, opens the back door and yells out to him.

"Ticky if you want me to braid yo hair you better come on! I got shit to do!"

"Can't you see I'm tending to my bitch right now! I'll be in there when I'm done."

"You keep on that'll be the only bitch you'll have to attend to!" Ticky waves her off. As he soaps Ms. Bitch up, he sees Terry walking through the alley. Terry is a smoked-out prostitute who used to be a bad bitch back in the day with a banging body. She was a student in college studying to be a nurse. But when her four-year-old daughter got killed by a stray bullet while playing on the porch, she lost it mentally and turned to the pipe to help her cope. After she turned to the pipe, she lost her banging body and good looks. Her breast that used to sit up like two big cantaloupes. Now, they looked like deflated hot water bags that hung down to her stomach. That ass that niggas used to break their necks to get a look at no matter how many times they saw it, was nothing more than tailbone now. And her beautiful yellow face was now sunken in and further added to her malnourished look. But in her mind, she still thinks she's that same bad bitch she used to be.

"Aye Terry!" Ticky yells catching her attention right away. She stopped in her tracks and looked over at him.

"Who is that? Ticky, that's you back there?"

"Yea, come here," he says waving her over. She walks over switching her boney ass so hard her whole body jerked with every switch.

"What's up, Tic Tic?" Ticky could tell she was high as an astronaut.

"You feeling good. Who you copped from?"

"I ain't copped this. I hitched hiked this ride to the moon. One of my friends gave me a hit of some shit they had got from a dealer they mess with. I can't lie, I'm high as hell. I've been high Ticky for over thirty minutes and ain't came down yet. Whoever Rick James copping this shit from got some straight drop."

"Did you say, Rick James? That's who gave you that shit?"

"Yea, Ricky Baby looked out for me."

"Listen, I'm going to get you some more of that shit alright."

"For real, Ticky?"

"Yea, but first go in the house and get you something to eat. You look like you ain't ate in days."

"Okay." She goes into the house. Ticky always took care of Terry. She was the only dope fiend he had a soft spot in his heart for. Not just because of what happened to her daughter, but because it was his bullet that killed her.

A few years ago, he and Truth were beefing with some niggas from Uptown who came and setup shop on Terry's end of the block. Him, Truth, and a few others from their squad went to holla at the niggas and get them to move around or pay block taxes, but those Uptown niggas wasn't trying to hear that. A simple attempt at getting an understanding turned to an argument quick. Then out of nowhere, one of the seven niggas that stood out there upped their heat and all hell broke loose. Shots rang out from all over the block as they spread out shooting. Ticky didn't even run for cover. He just walked down the street busting knocking niggas off one by one. He caught some movement on a nearby porch. Assuming it's one of his oppositions, he sent a shot its way. He heard the body fall with a light thud. When the smoke cleared, four of their niggas were dead and two of Ticky's boys were dead and two others with minor gunshot wounds to their arm and leg. But the scream that Ticky heard next still haunts him to this day. It was the horrific shrill of Terry finding her daughter, Erica, lying on the porch choking on her own blood before dying in her arms. A bullet had hit her in the neck and ruptured her jugular vein. Her blood covered Terry's blue nursing uniform. Her little hazel eyes stared up at her mama, but her soul was nowhere left in them. That day, Terry died in the inside along with Erica.

Ticky parks his midnight blue Dodge Ram truck across the streets from a four-unit apartment building on 1st and Keefe. "You sure this is Rick James's crib?"

"I'm positive. I would forget my name before I ever forget where I got a high that good at."

"Grab you some get right, but chill for a while. I want to peep the scene out here for a little bit."

"How long is a little while?"

"As long as this last you." He gives her a hundred-dollar bill and her eyes get big.

"That's why you my mothafuck'n nigga!" She kisses him on the jaw and hurries out the door.

"Terry don't forget. I wanna know who all be in there, what they be doing, and how much work they be having in there."

"I got you." She switches her ass speedily across the street and rings the doorbell. A voice comes through the intercom.

"Who is it?"

"It's Terry." Moments later, she's buzzed into the building. Ticky sat back with his Draco in his lap and watched the building. It didn't take long before he started seeing all the traffic that comes to the building. Most, if not all, was his customers. He was starting to get pissed when he guesstimated in his head how much money whoever Rick James was housing was taking off his plate. It took everything in him to fight off the urge of running up in there with the Draco and laying everybody in the house down. Just as he was fighting off that urge a tall skinny red nigga with a fitted cap and white T-shirt walks up to the building talking on the phone. Rick James meets him at the door and they both disappear inside.

"Deadman walking," Ticky says to himself, having a feeling that that had to been the nigga that he's been looking for. As soon as Terry gives him the conformation, he promised to take all the animation out on that dead man.

Inside, Terry breaks down her 8-ball into twenty dime-size rocks and begins loading her pipe. She takes a hit and passes the pipe to Rick James. "Time to get high, baby," he says before sparking his torch and melting down the remainder of rock inside the pipe into smoke, that he inhaled greedily into his lungs. His phone rings. He passes the pipe back to Terry and answers the phone while blowing out a breath of smoke. "Hello."

"Come open the door."

"I'm on my way, baby." Rick James puts his phone on the table. "Here comes the blessings, baby!" He goes to open the lobby door for his visitor. Moments later, he returns with Do-Dirty.

"Get yo ass off that video game, lil nigga, and let's count this money."

"Damn, hold on Do-Dirty. You can't just pause when you playing Call Of Duty live online. I'll get my troops killed."

Do-Dirty walks over and turns off the TV. "Man, what the fuck!"

"Nigga, fuck yo game. Go get my mothafuck'n money." Tank tosses down the game controller and storms off to the back to grab the money from the stash spot. Do-Dirty goes into the kitchen and Terry leans over and whispers to Rick James.

"Ricky, who is that?" she asks, seeking information to take back to Ticky.

"That's my mans, Do-Dirty. He the one who supplies us with this good good." He leans a little closer and whispers to her a little lower. "And he loves to take some of the ladies to the backroom for a good time."

"Shit, as long as he breaks me off some of that good dope, I'm down with that."

"I hear you, baby. But you know all good things must come with a blessing for ol' Rick James now," he says as he lights his pipe. She slides him one of her rocks.

"Set it up." She needed a way to check out that backroom they kept locked. She wanted to return to Ticky with as much useful information she could get her ears and eyes on.

She thought of Ticky as her homeboy and one of the only dealers she truly respected. He was always there for her and making sure she was straight. He was one of the only and few people that were in her corner after Erica died. And for that, he forever had her loyalty.

It was of no doubt to her that Ticky was going to kill that nigga, Do-Dirty, for setting up shop over there.

She knew Ticky had a wild temper. She also knew he was no fool. He wasn't going to let no good dope make it to the police evidence locker when he could easily take it for himself. He was going to rob that nigga first and then kill him. She knew when all was said and done, he would hit her hand real good for all her help. So, she knew she had to get as much information as she could possibly get.

Selling out of the nine ounces in two days that they brought down to Georgia, Noodles and Pay Pay got back into town last night and now they were sitting at Baby Red's kitchen table giving him the rundown on how things went.

"Damn! nine ounces in two days?"

"Bro I'm telling you they love this shit out there! We're still getting calls from down there asking when we'll be back," Noodles says, just as excited as Baby Red was. Pay Pay slams his hand on the table.

"We got to go back down there with a whole lot more than nine ounces this time. I'm talking about at least a brick or two. If not, we just going to be right back here in a few days picking up some more."

"That shit sounds beautiful, my nigga, if things could pan out like that. But I don't know about that one Pay Pay. That's a lot of work to be hauling down to an unfamiliar city. Anything could happen. And that much work, that would have to come out of Billy Gunz's stash. Like I said I don't know. That's a lot of risks to be taking."

"Think about it, that's a lot of risks to be taking coming back and forth when we can just go down there with a heavy load and sit straight for a little while." Paris walks in the house sets her keys on the table and gives Baby Red a kiss. He pulls her down onto his lap.

"Help me out on something, baby."

"What?" He breaks down the whole dilemma he was having with the team.

"What you think I should do?" Paris gets up and rounds up all the dope they have left in the house and sets it on the table.

"We have four and a half keys left. It would take us about a little over two weeks to get off one whole key. If they getting rid of nine ounces in two days, then I say hit them with two bricks and see them in sixteen days," she says sliding Pay Pay and Noodles each a brick. She looks over at Baby Red to see if he had something to say about the decision she just made. He puts his hands up surrendering to her decision.

"The queen has spoken."

The last few days things between Pay Pay and Noodles had been weird. After waking up the morning after their drunken love affair and promising to never tell anyone what happen the night before, every attempt at a one on one conversation turned awkward. The whole trip back from Georgia they barely shared more than a few words with each other. The silence in the car was filled by the sounds of music. And now they were back in the car, just the two of them following Classy back to Georgia.

King Dream

~ CHAPTER 10 ~

Terry runs across the street and gets into Ticky's truck. "You got the info I need?"

"I got everything I can get."

"Talk to me." He starts the truck up and pulls off. She lights a cigarette.

"Well, the nigga that's setting up shop is a dude named Do-Dirty."

"Do-Dirty? What he look like?"

"Tall, skinny, and red."

"Was he wearing a fitted cap and a white T-shirt?"

"Yup! That's him."

"I just saw that nigga come and go from here."

"Yea, he came to drop off some more dope."

"How many niggas he got in there working?"

"Just some lil kid. A lil nigga no more than thirteen maybe fourteen years old. Do-Dirty drops him off quarter ounces to hustle. He just came by tonight and dropped some off." She rolls down her window a crack and dumps the cigarette ash.

"Just one lil nigga, huh? That shouldn't be hard getting past him. Who is the nigga Do-Dirty getting his dope from?"

"That one I couldn't find out. But I know Do-Dirty is pushing some heavyweight himself. I heard him on the phone with somebody saying he only had half a bird left." Ticky rubs his chin as the wheels in his mind turn.

"Did you get a good layout of the apartment?"

"Sure did. They're downstairs in Apartment Two. It's laid out like this." She turns sideways in her seat to face him. "As you walk through the front door of the apartment, it's the living room. In the living room, there's one long couch, a coffee table, a sofa chair, TV, and all that shit. There are two windows in the living room that can be accessed from the side of the building. You turn left into the hall and right away on your next left is the kitchen. Go down the hall some more and on your right is the bathroom. Go down the hall some more and there's a room on your left and on your right. The one on the left is Rick James' room. It's setup like an average bedroom with a bedroom set and all that. The room on the right is the one that's always locked. That's where they keep their dope and money. In there, it's a bedroom set and all that too, but in the closet is a small portable safe they keep everything in."

"If that room is always locked, then how did you get in there and see all that?" She smacks her lips.

"Can't no nigga resist my fine ass! Or the opportunity for a ride in the bed on this thoroughbred! Me and Do-Dirty did a dope date and when we finished, I took a hit off my pipe. While I was smoking, he went into the closet and took some money out of the safe. But as he went deeper off into the closet to hide the safe, I bust a move for you."

"You bust a move for me? What kind of move?"

"I snuck over to the other side of the room and unlocked one of the windows for you. With the window facing the alleyway, it's easy access for you to get in and out without being seen."

"That's what I'm talking about. That was quick thinking. I'm going to take care of you again tomorrow. But I need you to do one more thing for me."

The bicycle horn screams repeatedly as people curse and move out of the way of the speeding bike. "Move bitches, get out the way! Rick James got to get to his blessing, baby!" he says as he speeds down the sidewalk on his bike and comes to a skidding stop in front of Ticky's house. He hops off the bike letting it fall to the ground, then runs onto the porch and knocks on the door. Ticky answers the door and sees him bent over trying to catch his breath. "Ticky, tell me Terry ass wasn't lying when she told me what she told me."

"What she tell you?" Rick James stands straight up, but still breathing hard.

"She said you had a quarter ounce blessing for me if I was to come right away and bust a move for you."

"Yea, you got the right message. Come on in." He follows him into the house rubbing his hands together. Conscious and well alert this time of the reach of the dogs, he moves far too the left as he enters the living room area. But surprisingly, the dog wasn't there. None of them were.

"What you get rid of all your dogs or something?" he asks, looking all-around of him and seeing no sign of them.

"Nah, it's feeding time. I don't like to feed them in here. You know how messy dogs can be when they feast."

"I don't know, me and dogs don't get along. I'm a cat person myself." Ticky leads him through the kitchen to a back door that led to the basement. Going down the steps, he begins to develop a strange feeling in the pit of his stomach. "Um Ticky, what exactly it is you need me to do?"

"Just follow me." That strange feeling grew stronger with every step he took. Everything in his experience told him it's never a good idea to follow a mothafucka as crazy as Ticky into a basement. Not being able to ignore his gut feeling any longer, he stopped halfway down the steps.

"You know what? I'll be right back. I got to go put my bike on the porch before somebody tries to steal it." He turns around quickly and heads back up the steps, but Dee Dee was right at the doorway with the chopper around her neck as usual, and this time she had her finger on the trigger.

"No, no, take yo ass back down them steps." Rick James knew then what was waiting for him downstairs was far from the blessing he was looking for.

***

Baby Red was making way back to the Mil after making another run with Missy down to Georgia. As usual, it was like the preacher was talking about him. The day's sermon came from Proverbs Chapter 9:6: *Forsake the foolish, and live; and go in the way of understanding...*

Which was wisdom he didn't think he would need so soon when his phone rang. "Yea."

"Nigga, I warned yo ass about yo cousin stepping on my toes!" Baby Red takes the phone away from his ear and looks at it strangely before putting it back to his ear.

"First off, take that bass out yo voice when you talk to me. Secondly, Booth Street ain't part of your turf, nigga. That's free game over there."

"Fuck Booth Street. I ain't talking about that. You can't tell me you're ignorant to what Do-Dirty's been doing."

"What you talking about?"

"He setup shop at Rick James' place over on First and Keefe."

"That's a lie. Do-Dirty been working the spot on Booth. And I know this for a fact because I pop up randomly and he's always there, so whoever is supplying you with this information is bullshitting you. Because a nigga can't be in two places at once."

"Ticky told me and everybody knows Ticky don't bullshit. He don't swear to shit. He can't prove. You want to keep playing dumb to your cousin's moves, then that's your problem. Him putting his hand in my pockets is my problem. I gave you fair warning about this shit last time, so to solve the issue this time, I'm airing his ass out when I see him. If that brings beef between you and I, then let's put that shit on the stove.

Because me and my niggas is always ready to cook some shit up." Truth hangs the phone up before Baby Red could snap out a reply.

"Damn Dirt!" he yells out loud. He might've tried to take up for Do-Dirty on the phone with Truth, but he knew what Truth was saying had to be true. Do-Dirty has been running through work a lot faster than normal and has been too busy to get on his nerves like usual.

It was no talking Truth out of it this time. Do-Dirty's greed and superiority complex has finally crossed the line. Truth wasn't going to let the shit slide and Baby Red wasn't going to let anything happen to his cousin, so now war was inevitable.

***

"Yea, Ticky. I got the layout... I'm in the alley now...I know take everything and meet you back at the house, got it...Alright bye." Roach, one of Ticky's workers, slides his phone back in his pocket then creeps to the bedroom window of Rick James' apartment.

He puts his ear to the window to listen and see if anyone was in there. It was silent. He tried the window, and just like Terry reported, it was unlocked. As he slowly raised the window, headlights slowly crept down the alleyway causing Roach to abandon the window and take cover in the bushes next door. Just like he thought, only police crept that slow. The squad car slowly went by and then made a left turn out of the alley. Roach came out of his hiding place and continued his mission. Once the window was open, he slowly pulled back the curtains. The room was dark with the only illumination coming from a digital alarm clock that sat on a nightstand next to the bed. But Roach could tell there wasn't anyone in the room. And moments later, he was inside.

"Watch yo back nigga!" Bullets scream through the air making him take cover at a nearby building. He cocks back his Desert Eagle and returns four shots just before a parade of rapid-fire spits back at him. "Damn can I get some fucking help out here!" He tries to return fire, but his pistol is out of ammunition. He reaches for the clip to reload, but it was too late. A multitude of bullets rains down on him leaving him drowning in a pool of his own blood. "Damn!" Tank says snatching his headset off his head and throwing it down along with the controller. Just as he did so the doorbell rang. He exhales a heavy breath of irritation then gets up and answers the intercom. "What!"

"It's Freddie, I need four of them thang thangs." He buzzes him in. Freddie makes it to the apartment door and Tank lets him in. "Let me get four fat ones, nephew." Tank opens his sack and sees he only has two left.

"Wait here, I got to grab some more from the back." He goes to the backroom to get another sack. He unlocks the door and when he walks in, he sees the window wide open and a nigga rambling through the closet. The nigga stops rummaging through the closet when he notices someone walked into the room. Their eyes lock for a second, then Tank pulls his strap out. He squeezes the trigger ready to blow the nigga's top back, but nothing happens. He squeezes again and still nothing more than a click.

"You forgot about the safety switch, lil nigga," Roach says, then with one swift motion pulls out his strap and quickly send three shot to his chest. Tank's body jerked as each shot hit him. He slowly fell to his knees. Not believing what just happened was real, he touches one of the wounds on his chest and sees the blood on his fingers. Roach tries to fire another shot, but the gun jammed. As he tries to unjam it, Tank hits the safety switch and send two bullets his way. One strikes him in the chest and the last one hit him dead in the center of his forehead. Roach fell to the floor dead. Tank smiled with pride at how accurate his aim was and then the gun fell from his hand; he falls over dead.

King Dream

~ CHAPTER 11 ~

Blood dripped from his mouth and nose, forming red stripes down his white Newport cigarettes shirt as he sat tied to a chair in the basement. He was surrounded by eight vicious pit bulls chained to the wall. One of them a huge red nose pitbull with one eye missing was the one that scared him the most. Ticky called him Lucifer. He was like the leader of the pack. He was known to break loose from his chains and try to kill everything he could sink his teeth into.

"I treated you good, Rick James. When you asked for a blessing, I gave you one. And to pay me back for all my generosity, you lie to me and help the next man take food off MY TABLE!" With a dog chained wrapped around his hand Ticky sends his fist flying right into Rick James's mouth.

"OHHH!" he moans as he leans over to the side and spits out his two front teeth. Lucifer charges at him from one side of his chair and was snatched back by the chain he was hooked to, but not before taking a piece of his shirt with him. As Rick James leans away from Lucifer, Ms. Bitch charges from the other side and snatches off a piece of his blue windbreaker pants. "Come on Ticky man! Get these crazy-ass dogs!"

"I told you to stay still." Ticky unwraps the chain from around his hand and walks into another room in the basement. Moments later, he comes out with the biggest and meanest looking dog Rick James had ever laid his eyes on.

"If you think Lucifer and Ms. Bitch is crazy, meet their son, Six." The huge red brindle beast growled and snarled like a hound from hell. Thick globs of foam and slob dripped from his mouth as he barked and snapped. As big and stocky as Ticky was, he could barely hold on to Six. The dog kept jerking him every time it launches towards Rick James. Rick James almost pissed his pants. He could've sworn that at any moment Six was going to break loose from Ticky's hold. "This evil mothafucka here hate everything moving. He's the one responsible for Lucifer's missing eye. He loves the taste of fresh blood. Ain't that right boy!" Six launched forward even harder this time coming just inches from Rick James's face.

"Come on Ticky man! I'm sorry! Tell me, tell me, how can we make this right?" he pleads through his now missing two front teeth.

"You want to make this right?" Truth says coming down the basement stairs. "Tell us all you know about Do-Dirty and his cousin Baby Red's operation."

"Come on baby, I can tell you all about how Do-Dirty moves, but I don't know much about Red's business... Damn, I need a blessing," he says with tears in his eyes and a sob in his voice.

"Calm down," Truth says as he unties him. "Here, get your smoke on and calm your nerves." He passes him a fat rock of dope. Rick James loads it into his pipe and puts his torch to it. It wasn't like the dope he was used to getting from Do-Dirty, but to him, anything was better than nothing at that moment. "You good now?"

"Yea, I'm good."

"Then tell us what all it is you know."

"I know Do-Dirty has a spot at Mookie's house over on Booth Street. That's where he keeps the majority of his work."

"How much work we talking?"

"Well from the conversations I overheard him having with Baby Red, I'll say at least a brick."

"Damn, a whole chicken. Who are they getting this work from?"

"That I don't know."

"Come on Ricky help me out better than that. Do you at least know where in the house he keeps his work?"

"Yea, now that one I can answer. He keeps it somewhere in the attic along with the money. Now, I don't know where at up there because Do-Dirty keeps it locked and no one is allowed up there. And he walks around that bitch with two fat ass 45's. If a mothafucka even touch that doorknob, he lighting they ass up like a Christmas tree."

"Who mans the spot with him?"

"It used to be some nigga and a stud chick, but Do-Dirty moved them around, so it's just him and Mookie there. And that's all I know, I swear."

"Relax, you gave us everything we needed." Truth headed toward the stairs.

"So, I can go now, right?"

"Yea, you can go. Go straight to hell mothafucka. Six feasts!" Ticky unhooked the leash and Six launched towards Rick James grabbing him by his side. With his mouth locked on to him, he begins shaking Rick James like a ragdoll. He fell to the floor screaming putting himself in the reach of the other dogs. They all begin to feast on him like a pack of hungry wolves. His screams excited the dogs even more making them bite and shake even harder. And in only a matter of minutes, his screams became silent as God gave him his last blessing. The blessing of death.

Do-Dirty pulls up on Rick James' block but sees the police had it taped off. "What the fuck is going on over here?" he says to himself. He parks on the next block and walks back around. People in the neighborhood stood around watching everything that was going on. Do-Dirty turns to one of the people standing out there. "Say bruh, what's all this about?"

"Man, they say two niggas got popped in there."

"You know what apartment?"

"Dope fiend Freddie says it was Rick James's apartment. He said some lil nigga name Dank or Tank or something like that and some other nigga shot it out in there and killed each other."

"How he know?"

"The nigga say he was in the house when everything was going down." A heavyset woman pulls up to the scene in a station wagon and hops out. Do-Dirty knew exactly who she was. She runs under the yellow tape just as the coroners were wheeling out the bodies. A police officer grabbed her before she could get too close.

"Let me go. I need to know if that's my baby! Is that Tank!" She breaks free from the officer's hold and rushes over and before the other officers or coroners could stop her, she was able to unveil both bodies. Seeing Tank's lifeless body lying on the stretcher, she screamed as loud as she could and tried to wrap her arms around him, but the police pulled her away kicking and screaming.

Do-Dirty turned to the man next to him again. "Anybody know where Rick James is?"

"Hell nah, ain't nobody seen him since early this morning."

"You know where I can find Freddie?"

"Probably at his crib on Hubbard Street smoking all that dope he found in Rick James's apartment."

Do-Dirty walks back to his car and pulls off, headed for Freddie's house.

Freddie sat on a dirty air mattress in the living room with Samantha. Samantha is a white dope fiend from around the way that he considers his woman. But she only comes around to pay him attention when he has something to smoke or some money to spend on something to smoke. Samantha took a hit of the pipe and started sucking her tongue. "I told you, I had some fire shit. Got you tasting your tongue it's so good. Now pass it back." She passes it to him. His eyes grow big as he sucks in his hit. He bobs his head from side to side. "That's what I'm talking about. Woo, it's getting hot in here." He takes his shirt off and wipes the sweat from his forehead.

"Let me and Debbie get some of that Freddie," Kyle says sitting on a crate on the other side of the room next to his girl-friend, Debbie.

"Where y'all money at?" he asks while cleaning out his pipe so he could load another hit. Debbie put her hand on her hip.

"How you gonna charge us after we smoked our dope with you last night and this morning?"

"Mothafucka, that bunk ass dope y'all shared. That shit was more cut than dope. Hell, if I wanted to smoke baking soda, I just get some out the refrigerator."

"It's the thought that counts."

"Well bitch, you need to stop thinking. Besides, I can't be giving out no dope. Me and my baby finna start getting this money. Ain't that right, baby?" He kisses Samantha on the cheek, and she nods her head yes as she takes another blast. Kyle and Debbie put some money together and Kyle walks over to Freddie.

"You don't know anything about getting no money, Freddie. I don't know where you got all that dope and money from you got right now. But I bet you going smoke it all up in a week and be back going in on sacks of dope with us."

"Until then, that will be ten dollars a hit if you want some of this shit." Someone knocks at the back door. "Samantha go answer the door. That might be a customer." She goes to the door and when she opens it, she's met with the barrel of Do-Dirty's 45. Even if she was to take the greatest blast ever from her pipe her eyes couldn't get any wider than they did right then.

"Where is Freddie?" He whispered to her with a mug on his face as he steps inside. She points behind her to the front room. He waves his gun at her signaling for her to lead him to him. He closes the door behind him and follows her into the front room.

"Baby who was that at the -" He stopped in mid-sentence when he saw Do-Dirty Standing there holding a gun. All three of them froze when they saw him.

"Which one of you niggas is Freddie?" Everybody pointed at Freddie.

"What do you want with me?"

"Who was that nigga that ran in Rick James' spot today and killed Tank?"

"I don't know what you talking about. I wasn't there." Do-Dirty cocks back the 45 and shoots a shot off, landing the round inches away from Freddie and into the air mattress. The air seeps quickly out of the mattress sinking him to the floor.

"His name is Roach. He is one of Truth's and Ticky's goons," he answers quickly, seeing Do-Dirty wasn't going to play with him.

"Who the fuck is Ticky?"

"He's Truth's business partner. They are like each other's right-hand man. He lives over on Palmer and Center Street."

"Alright, one more thing."

"What?"

"Where the fuck is my money and dope?"

"Now that part I don't know. I swear on my mama I don't know shit about no money and dope." Debbie and Kyle point to a lamp that sat next to Freddie. "Ain't that about a bitch," he says looking at Debbie and Kyle with disappointment. Do-Dirty turns the lamp upside down and removes the bottom cover. He pulls out two ounces along with a quarter bagged up in dimes, plus four G's and some change in cash. The two ounces and four G's was what he kept in the safe at Rick James' house. He kept that there for emergencies, in case anything happened with the shit he had at Mookie's spot, he would have something to fall back on. He puts the money in his pocket and stuff the two ounces in his draws He then points the gun back in Freddie's face.

"I'll take the rest of that money you took too." Freddie shakes his head. He digs and his pocket and hands him the money he took out of Tank's pockets. Do-Dirty counts it and sees it's all there. He proceeded to slap Freddie across the face with the pistol. "Next time don't make shit so hard." He falls to the side holding his face.

"Um, before you go, can I buy a couple of those bags from you? I got eighteen dollars. Three of it is in quarters though," Debbie says. Do-Dirty pulls fifteen dime bags out of the quarter ounce sack and gives Debbie, Kyle, and Samantha each five. "That's on me for all your cooperation."

"What about me?" Freddie ask.

"Be happy I'm letting you live." Do-Dirty leaves out the back door.

The three of them load their pipes up and take hits. "Samantha, let me get a hit baby." She shakes her head no. "No? How you going to tell me no when you just got through smoking off me?" She shrugs her shoulders. He looks over at Debbie and Kyle. "Kyle, Debbie, let me get a lil hit."

"Nope."

"I thought we were better than that."

"I'ma tell you like you told me. Well, bitch, you need to stop thinking," Debbie says as she blows a cloud of smoke in his face.

King Dream

~ CHAPTER 12 ~

Do-Dirty walks into Mookie's and before he could take his hat off, he's slammed into the wall so hard it nearly knocks the wind out his chest. "You just couldn't resist kicking off some bullshit huh? I let you talk me into letting you setup shop over here. Even let you run things *yo way*! But you still had to go and setup shop on Truth's turf! Why Dirt?"

"What the fuck is you talking about?" Do-Dirty knows Truth must've had given word to Baby Red about him setting up shop at Rick James', but he plays stupid to gain his innocence in Baby Red's eyes.

"Stop playing with me, Dirt! Truth already told me you opened up shop at Rick James's spot!"

"This may sound like an oxymoron to you, but Truth is a goddamn lie! Rick James had some other niggas in there serving. If you don't believe me, check the news." He nods his head towards the TV in the living room. Baby Red releases his grip on him and walks over and turns the TV on. He flips it to the news. The news stations switched their feed to a reporter in the field that stood outside of Rick James' apartment building. Baby Red turns the volume up on the TV.

"Today, a double homicide occurred at this building here behind me on the 3400 block of East 1st Street. It is the outcome, authorities say, of a drug deal gone wrong where both suspects killed each other in the midst. The victims' and suspects' names at this moment are being withheld until further investigation and the owner of the apartment can be located for questioning. One of the suspects was as young as fourteen years old. A sad reality to the lives of today's youth. I'm Marsha Johnson with *WMX Channel 4 News*. Back to you, Alex." Baby Red shuts off the TV.

"I told you. That nigga Truth is just mad we eating more than he is out here. And because of that, he wants to try and turn us against each other," he says sparking a blunt to calm his nerves and watches Baby Red's reaction to what he just said. Baby Red rubs his forehead as if trying to stop a headache from approaching.

"Damn. This shit is finna get ugly, Dirt. Real ugly real fast. That nigga Truth wants you dead. And if I get in the way, then he's at my head too. This puts all of our lives in jeopardy and kills our hustle," he says calmly with his hands clasped together and his chin resting on top staring off into his thoughts as if he was picturing what was to come.

"So, what you going to do?" Baby Red could hear the wonder and worry in his voice. The wonder if he was going to turn his back on him and the worry what he was going to do if he did. Baby Red was all the family he had left.

"Look Dirt, I'm -"

Boom! Boom! Boom!

Before Baby Red could give him an answer, bullets tore through the house, shattering glass and landing into the walls sending thick clouds of drywall dust floating in the air.

When the procession of shots stopped, both Baby Red and Do-Dirty grabbed their heaters and ran to the window. Peeping out they see two of Truth and Ticky's goons getting back in the car they came in. Baby Red and Do-Dirty ran out the door, busting at the car as it sped off. Do-Dirty looks over at Baby Red. "I guess now you ain't got no choice."

"I was going to ride with you anyway, fool."

Noodles sat on her bed in the hotel room with a tray on her lap bagging up zips of dope. She tries to ignore Pay Pay's constant glances at her, looking as if he wanted to say something but doesn't know how.

He does it again, but this time she's had enough of the tension and awkwardness that sat between them. She puts the tray to the side and turns his direction. "What? What is it Pay Pay? Just please say it already! You have been sitting there counting that same stack of money for the last twenty minutes. What?" Pay Pay tosses the money to the side and stands up to confront her.

"You tell me what it is! This is our third trip out here and ever since our first one, you've been acting real funny towards me. We don't talk or kick it like we used to and you always doing everything you can not to be alone with me. And when we are alone, it's like you go into your own little world." She jumps up to faceoff with him.

"How the fuck you expect for me to act when we crossed lines we shouldn't have crossed? We can't go back from that!"

"Then we move forward!"

"Forward? What you mean, like me and you in a relationship or something?"

"Why not?"

"Why not? Because I'm a fucking lesbian that's why not. I like women and only women!"

"That's not what I saw that night."

"I was drunk! What happened that night was a drunken mistake, so get over it!"

"Stop fronting, we both know that ain't true. In fact, this whole dike shit you on is just an illusion. It's nothing more than a defense mechanism you created after you got gangraped in middle school!" Noodles not wanting to hear anymore. Pained at the memory his words held, she swung off on Pay Pay, catching him in the jaw. She swings, again and again, hitting him in the chest until her fist became too heavy to swing. Pay Pay stood there and took every hit. Then held her close as she broke down into tears.

"That's right, baby. Let that shit out. You ain't got nothing to be afraid no more. I got you."

He read her like a book. It was no secret what had happened to her in the eighth grade. Everybody growing up with them around that time heard about her getting gang-raped in the boiler room of the school. A boy she liked along with two of his friends lead her down there for what they told her was going to be a smoke session. The smoke session turned out to be them pinning her down and stripping her of her innocence. The story had made the news. Even though her name was withheld from the newspapers and news reports, the word still got out that she was the victim.

Ever since then she never trusted being with a man. and never trusted herself being a woman. She started dressing like a thug and dating women, using her newly found masculinity as a defense mechanism to cover up the pain she felt inside. Also, to give her a false sense of strength to cover for the power she felt she had lost.

He scoops her up off her feet and lays her on the bed. "Why do you want me, Pay Pay? I'm damaged goods." He rubs his hand down the side of her face.

"That's not the way I see it."

"What is it that you see?"

"A woman. A woman who had her share of pain in life like any other black person growing up in the ghetto. We all got our soul wounds that left us with some type of scar or another. You just got to stop letting your scars define your beauty. Once you could do that, your past loses its control over you and you take back all the power your loss." He cuffs her chin in his hand forcing her to look up at him. "And most of all, when I see you, I see the woman that I love and want to be mines." A brief moment of silence took its attendance in the room as Noodles thought about the things he was saying. Not wanting to fight her feelings for him anymore, she gives in. Completely submitting herself to him.

"I love you too." Her lips pressed against his and they find themselves right back in each other's lustful embrace.

It was ten o'clock in the morning and the house was so hot the walls sweated. Do-Dirty sat at the kitchen table with one plate of powder and another one with some dope he just rocked up on the stove. With a cigarette in his mouth and a razor blade in hand, he chopped chunks of crack rock into dime and dubs.

Mookie walks into the kitchen fanning herself. "Damn, this got to be the hottest day of the summer." She opens the refrigerator. Inside was damn near empty except for a box of baking soda, a milk jug filled with tap water, half a carton of eggs, a half-eaten bowl of Ramen Noodles, and an open pack of hotdogs. She pulls out the jug of water pours her some in an empty pickle jar. She puts the jug back and closes the refrigerator door. She takes a seat at the table.

"Don't trip, I'm going to let you clean the plate when I'm done," Do-Dirty tells her. Mookie loved scraping together all the left-over residue off the plates so she could smoke it. And Do-Dirty always left her with something extra on the plates when he got done bagging up.

"I know you won't forget about me. That ain't what I came in here for." She takes a sip of her water.

"Then tell me what's up because I can do without all the extra body heat in here."

"I wanted to see if you heard what happen to yo boy, Rick James." He stopped chopping dope and looked up at her.

"What happened to Rick James?"

"Word is a city worker found him in a sewer dead. They said his body was ripped to shreds like some animal or pack of dogs ate his ass up. It was so bad they had to identify him by his dental records." She takes another sip of water and sits the glass down then starts fanning herself. "No wonder why this kitchen is hotter than the rest of the house. You got this fan off." She reaches over to turn the fan on but stopped in her tracks when Do-Dirty upped heat on her.

"Bitch, you turn that fan on and I'm going to push yo wig back. You see all this powder on the table."

"My bad, Do-Dirty," she says holding her hands up. He sits the gun back down on the table.

"Get yo ass out the kitchen, Mookie, until I'm done before you end up costing money." She gets up and leaves. Do-Dirty drops his cigarette butt into an empty Arizona Tea can.

He knew Rick James' death was the doings of Truth and Ticky. He also knew it was more of a message to him than it was to poor ol' Rick James. It was their way of letting him know he was next.

***

They pull into the parking lot of Club Swag and parked next to Pay Pay's Tahoe truck where the rest of the crew stood. Baby Red and Paris hop out their car and walk over to them. "What it do, my niggas?" Baby Red says as he shakes up with everybody.

"Shit, just been waiting on y'all slow ass to show up," Wee Wee says.

"Tell that to the beauty queen who spent almost two hours in the bathroom."

"To look this good takes time and attention," Paris says with a matter-of-fact tone and her hand on her hip.

"I think you should check yo makeup. You got some shit running down your face." Paris being the self-conscious type ran to the car and pulled down the visor to check herself out in the mirror.

Baby Red turns to his team. "Y'all remember not a word to Paris about the drama we have with Truth and Ticky. I don't need her worrying."

"Personally, I don't really give a fuck. But for the sake of curiosity, how long you think you going to be able to keep her in the dark? I'm sure it won't be long before Tokyo puts her on notice. I mean they do work at the same club," Do-Dirty says.

"I just want her to have a good time tonight then I'm going to let her know everything that's going on. In the meantime, everybody keep y'all eyes open. Security is going to be tight tonight. A bunch of off duty cops. It's going to be impossible to walk in there with our guns. Noodles, when we get in there go straight to the ladies' room. It's a window in there that only opens up a little bit. Not enough for a person to get through but enough for Pay Pay to pass you the guns from outside."

"I got you." Paris closes the car door and returns to Baby Red's side.

"Wasn't nothing wrong with my makeup."

"I see that didn't stop you from putting more on."

"Shut up and let's get in this club. My future baby daddy, Yo Gotti, is waiting on me," Paris says teasingly.

As they start walking out of the parking lot, Pay Pay pulls Baby Red to the side. "Have you lost your fucking mind? You don't tell wifey we got beef. On top of that, you have us all out here at a dope boy concert where all the dope boys in the city will sure to be in attendance. Including Truth and Ticky. What the fuck is you thinking?"

"Look, I'm showing these mothafuckas they don't put no fear in us and we damn sho ain't hiding. Besides, Paris had been waiting to go to this concert for a long time now. I'm not finna let Truth and Ticky's spoil her night. Like I said, I'm going to tell her everything tonight after the concert. Until then, stay on point and make sure you get them units to Noodles." Baby Red slaps a hand on Pay Pay's shoulder and leaves.

Pay Pay grabs the guns out the truck and slips around back to the bathroom window. He makes a bird call and seconds later the window rises up six inches where he hands the guns to Noodles. He leans his face into the opening and gives her a kiss. "Baby Red is being real reckless right now. We shouldn't even be here."

"Tell me about it. I've been having a bad feeling about this all night."

"You just stay close to me tonight, alright?"

"Alright."

~ CHAPTER 13 ~

Plies leaves the stage after performing his song, "Worth Going Feds For". Right away, Yo Gotti takes the stage flowing his song, "Errrbody". The whole club gets geeked up. Paris seemed to have been having the time of her life, but Baby Red and the rest of his crew were too busy staying on point. "Are you going to keep looking around the club or are you going to dance with me?"

"I am dancing."

"No, you're standing there like a zombie walking in place and looking all around the club. What's wrong?"

"Nothing. It's just a lot of people in here tonight. You know I don't like crowds like that."

"What you expect? My husband, Yo Gotti, is here."

"You keep playing with me you going to get you and Yo Gotti's ass fucked up." They both laugh.

Feeling a set of eyes on him he looks over at the bar area and sees Truth staring right at him. He looks over at his crew who is already on point. He points his head at Paris without her noticing and Noodles comes walking over. He leans down to Paris's ear. "I'm going to grab a drink, baby. Dance with Noodles for a little bit."

"Okay."

He walks over to the bar and stands side by side with Truth so he can keep his eyes on his surroundings as they talked. "Judging by the bullet holes in Mookie's house, I take it Do-Dirty got the message I sent. And seeing that he's over there with his hand under his shirt clutching that old ass 45, he knows it ain't no mo talking," he says pointing his drink at Do-Dirty was standing across the room.

"Yea, *we* got the message. But I promise you ain't going to like the reply."

"You know you could walk away from this, right? No reason you and I even got to go there. Do-Dirty's the one that brought shit to this level. My beef ain't with you."

"Walk away? Nahhh." He shakes his head. "You should know me well enough by now to know that ain't gon happen. I'm my brother's keeper, fo sho. I'm loyal 'til they lay me in the soil. So, you beef with Do-Dirty, you beef with me." Truth smirks at his reply.

"I figured you would feel that way. It's going to be a bloody summer."

"Then let's paint these streets red."

Yo Gotti switches to his song, "Down in the DM", and the crowd sings along. Noodles pretends to dance with Paris while keeping her eyes on Truth's niggas.

"I'll be back. I got to go to the bathroom!" Paris yells to her over the music.

"I'll go with you!" She follows her to the bathroom and after a quick flush, Paris walks out of the stall and washes her hands. Noodles pretends to wash hers. After drying her hands-off, Paris begins reapplying her makeup.

"Care to share with me how long you and Pay Pay have been fucking around?" she asks nonchalantly, catching Noodles off guard.

"Me and Pay Pay? What?" Paris looks over at her with a stop fronting look.

"You really going to play stupid with me?"

"It's that obvious?"

"To me, hell yea. Come on now, you two try too hard making it seem like y'all aren't together not to be." When it came to reading people, Paris was a professor in the art of it. It wasn't much that could get passed her. Noodles begins breaking it all down to her about her and Pay Pay.

Pay Pay went and posted up near the ladies' room when he saw Noodles and Paris head in there. Do-Dirty and Wee Wee stayed posted by their table watching Baby Red's back. "I hope all that money you made on Ticky and Truth's turf was worth this war," Wee Wee says, smoking on a cigarette.

"I ain't sold shit on their turf."

"Man, save yo interrogation defense. You ain't got to lie to me, I know the truth. My side bitch, Peaches, stays across the street from Rick James' apartment building. I've seen you myself over there doing yo thang."

"Then why haven't you exposed that to Baby Red and the rest of the crew?"

"Because I don't give a fuck. Truth's a bitch ass nigga in my book. I've been itching to go to war with the nigga so we could take over all his spots."

"Now that's what the fuck I've been talking about. If I would have known you thought like that, then you and I could've been moved that nigga around."

"Hell yea. He got some hittas though. They will bring it on the battlefield, but shit, I'm ready to wet all their asses up. The only nigga I'm worried about is Ticky."

"Why is mothafuckas so afraid of this Ticky nigga?"

"Because Ticky is a certified nutcase. That man is just as mad as the dogs he keeps and as merciless as Hitler." He takes a pull of his cigarette. "Damn, speaking of the devil." Wee Wee spots Ticky walking in and points to him with a nod of his head. As Ticky scans the club, Wee Wee slips his hand under his shirt and flips the safety switch off on his 9mm Ruger. He sees Truth leave the company of Baby Red and walk up to Ticky and whisper something in his ear. Ticky looks dead in their direction. In the next minute, his hand was under his shirt heading in their direction. "You better run or get yo heat ready because it's finna go down."

Paris puts her makeup away. "I'm happy for you and Pay Pay."

"Please Paris, don't tell Baby Red and the rest of them. We ain't ready for them to know."

"Don't trip; y'all secret is safe with me. But you need to tell me why everybody acting all paranoid tonight. And don't lie to me because I know something is up." Feeling guilty about keeping her in the dark about something so serious and knowing she wouldn't be able to live with herself if something was to happen to Paris that could've been avoided, if only she knew the danger that she was in. With those thoughts taking precedence in her mind, she told Paris everything. "That son of a bitch! Give me a gun. I know you always toting two of them, so give me one. I'm not finna be in this bitch without one." Noodles pass her a .380 from out her back pocket. As she yanks open the bathroom door, gunshots rang out in the club.

"GET DOWN!" Noodles pulls her back and they hit the floor. She pulls her Glock out. Moments later, the bathroom door flies open and both of them have their guns aimed at the door. They relax a little when they see it's Pay Pay.

"Pay Pay, where's Red?" Paris yells over the sound of gunshots.

"He's in there. I'll worry about him in a minute. Right now, I need to get y'all out of here." He smashes open the bathroom window with the butt of his gun. He tosses Noodles his truck keys. "Take my truck and y'all get out of here."

"What about you?"

"Don't worry about me. Just do what I told you. Now go!" Paris hurried out the window. Noodles turns and gives him a kiss. "Be careful."

"As much as possible. Go." She climbed out of the window and they ran to the truck.

It seems more than just Baby Red and his crew found a way to sneak their guns into the club. As Ticky was trying to get within shooting distance of Do-Dirty, a fight broke out in the club, and somebody ups a pistol and started busting. The whole club turned into a shooting gallery as Baby Red and his crew begins busting at Ticky, Truth, and their boys.

Yo Gotti and his entourage rushed off stage and out the backdoor of the club with pistols in hand. The people in the club scattered like roaches to the front door. Security called for backup not knowing who to shoot at. Baby Red took cover behind the bar. while Truth fired shots at him from a few tables away. On the other side of the room, Do-Dirty and Wee Wee took cover four tables apart from each other. Ticky fired shots at Do-Dirty from eight tables away, while one of his goons stood next to him firing shots at Wee Wee. Pay Pay crouched down in the hallway leading to the bathrooms firing shots at one of the niggas who was busting at him from the cover of a table near the stage. He dials Noodles phone in the midst.

"Yo, y'all straight?"

"Yea, we just sped out the parking lot and headed to Paris' house now."

"Good, we will meet y'all there." He slides the phone back in his pocket and knocks off two more shots catching his shooter in the ribs. The man falls over dead. Pay Pay checks his clip and then yells over to Baby Red. "My Clip is running low, we got to get the fuck out of here now!" Truth pop off two shots that went through the bar where Baby Red was crouched down at and nearly hit him in the face. Baby Red returns four shots back at him. "Head for the backdoor!" Another nigga comes busting shots at him from the other side of the bar. "Wee Wee, get this nigga off my ass!" Wee Wee catches his shooter with a shot to the chest and the man falls over.

"I'm on my way, my nigga." He stays low while moving from table to table to get closer to the shooter. He finds a good spot and takes aim. He catches the nigga slipping and sends a shot soaring through the air that penetrates through his ear knocking his brains on the floor. "Got em!"

The sounds of police cars start to become audible. Ticky whistles at Truth. "Truth, let's roll!" Truth and Ticky bust their way out the front door while Baby Red and his crew bust their way out the back. They jump in their rides and sped off.

Paris didn't smoke cigarettes, but she was so stressed that she bought a pack on the way home. And now, she was smoking her third one while pacing the floor with both anger and worry weighing deep on her. Noodles sat at the table hands shaking trying her hardest to control her own worrying.

They both jump when the front door opened up. A sigh of relief runs through both of them when they see everybody made it home in one piece.

Paris runs and wraps her arms around Baby Red. She squeezes him tight for a long moment as tears slid down her face. She breaks the embrace and slaps him so hard that it grabs everybody's attention.

"What the fuck were you thinking not telling me our lives in danger?" He turns his face back towards her.

"Because at the time it wasn't. Only Dirt's life was in danger."

"And what changed that? Because back at the club it seemed to be all our lives in danger." He didn't even have to answer. The look on his face told her everything. "Like always, you got in the middle of it. You won't be happy until Do-Dirty's stupid ass have us all lying in our graves!"

"I had no choice! What was I supposed to do? Let him kill my cousin?"

"Yes! That fool keeps getting into shit because he knows you are always going to bail him out. So yes, you should've let him reaped what he sowed. If not, you should've at least sent his ass out of state. But nah, you wouldn't do that because of your pride. So, I hope you happy because now you and Truth's pissing contest has become a matter of life and death. All our lives are at stake." She pushes past him, goes into the back room, and slams the door behind her. Baby Red turns to his crew to discuss their next move.

"Shit's finna get real nasty. With this war going on money is gonna slow down a lot. And getting it is going to come with a lot more obstacles than usual. So, Noodles and Pay Pay, I'm going to need y'all to keep doing y'all thang in Atlanta. I got twenty-five bricks. I'm going to send y'all there tomorrow with four of them. That should keep y'all good for a month."

"You think it's smart to keep more dope here than in Atlanta? You said it yo self. Money is going to slow down a lot with this war going on." Pay Pay says.

"I'm already taking a risk giving y'all four. Billy Gunz gets out in a week. About twenty-two of those twenty-five bricks belong to him. I got to have all his shit together when he comes home."

"And what happens when he comes home? When he sees this war you in out here, he ain't going to front you that much work anymore?"

"Then we'll buy what we can from him to stay in the game." Pay Pay shakes his head at him. "Wee Wee, I want you to holla at yo hookup and get us some more guns. Tell him we want some heavy shit. I want to show these niggas how we get down."

King Dream

~ CHAPTER 14 ~

It's been three days since the shootout at the dope boy concert. The past three days have been a bloodbath. Truth sent a hit squad to Pay Pay's spot in Uptown and killed everybody inside. Ticky ran up in Mookie's spot looking for Do-Dirty and the dope. When he saw there was no work left in the house and Mookie couldn't tell him where he could find Do-Dirty, he drowned her ass in a toilet full of piss for pissing him off. Baby Red retaliated by hitting three of Truth's spots and one of Ticky's, killing several of their men and taking what they could in the midst.

With everything going on, Baby Red had Paris to stop working at the club until the beef was over. He also had her change up how she moves along with making her change the places she frequently visits and the routes she takes. He also haves her driving around a minute to watch and see if anyone was following her before she comes home. But little did he know, she took her own safety measures on him by installing a tracking device on his phone. That way she knew where he was at all times.

Paris does her final decoy lap and confident that no one was following her, she heads home. She walks through the door with bags in hand. As soon as she closes the front door, someone grabs her from behind and puts their hand over her mouth and a gun to her head.

"You bet not say a word, bitch," he tells her. Another man wearing a Halloween mask and a hoodie comes out of the shadows of the hallway "Now, you're going to show us where the dope is and you better not try no funny shit or I'm going blow that pretty ass head of yours off. You understand me?" the lead man tells her. She shakes her head yes. He removes his hand from over her mouth and points the gun at the back of her head. Shaken and heart pounding, she leads them to the bedroom. Inside the bedroom closet, she removes a false wall and pulls out the keys of dope. The other man tosses her a duffle bag and she starts loading the dope inside it. "Where's the money at?" the lead man says, pointing the gun closer to her head.

"There ain't no money here. Baby Red made his drop today. That's all we got," she says balling up in the corner of the closet and covering her face with her hands. The other man grabs the duffle bag and slaps a hand on his partner's chest signaling for them to go. "It's yo lucky day, bitch," The lead man says, putting his gun away and running out the house.

Frightened and nervous, Paris grabs the gun Baby Red kept under the mattress and slowly went through every room in the house making sure the men were gone. She locks the house door and dialed Baby Red's number. No answer. "Come on, Baby Red, answer the phone." She calls several more times and no answer.

***

"What the hell you doing here, Classy?" Baby Red says walking into her hotel room.

"I missed you, baby." She wraps her arms around him. He breaks her embrace and peeps out the window. Lately, he's been paranoid because of everything that's been going on. On top of all that, he could swear that same blacked-out Dodge Challenger from Atlanta was there following him around Wisconsin. He hadn't slept in almost three days and it was taking its toll on him.

"You shouldn't be here. I told you it's too much drama going on right now."

"Your drama is in Milwaukee, this is Madison. A whole hour away from your troubles."

"Which is not far enough. What if somebody followed me here and found out you somebody close to me? They will kill you. This shit is real out here right now, Classy."

"I know that. I'm not some square ass White bitch that's lame to the street life. Don't let my semi- proper grammar and sweet side fool you, Baby Red. For the first twelve years of my life, I grew up in Grady Holmes projects. I was the only White girl in my neighborhood, so imagine that. I know how to take care of myself and I am a down ass bitch who's down to ride with you all the way." Baby Red exhales a deep breath and plops down on the bed.

"If you say so." She climbs on the bed and starts massaging his shoulders.

"You know what you need? You need some good loving and rest, and mamas got just what you need," she says before getting on her knees and burying her face in his lap.

After getting some superb head and knocking her back out, Baby Red rolled over and went to sleep. His phone rang in the pocket of his pants that laid on the floor. Classy grabs it, and ready to wake him up and give to him until she saw the caller ID said wifey with a picture of Paris. "I don't think so. It's my night tonight, bitch," she says to herself while turning off the ringer on the phone and slipping it back into his pants pocket. She proceeds to climb back in bed and lays on his chest.

They sit in the car on the next block as they watch the police tape off the crime scene of yet another one of their spots.

"We need to hurry up and put an end to these niggas, Ticky. We're losing way too much money and just as many soldiers as they are. I want that nigga, Baby Red, and Do-Dirty dead."

"I hear what you saying, Truth. Trust we going get these niggas off the map real soon. You just worry about Baby Red

I'ma take care of Do-Dirty by myself." Truth, having his feel of the scene, starts up the car and pulls off. His phone rings, he presses the hands-free button on the steering wheel and his caller is heard through the car speakers.

"What up, baby?"

"I got some good news for you, my love," Tokyo says on the other end

"Well talk it to me because I could really use it right now."

"I finally located that bitch, Paris. I caught her car flying down Center Street. I'm following her now. I'm sure she'll lead us to Baby Red. You find Baby Red, you're sure to find Do-Dirty too."

"That sounds like good news to me. Stay on her heels baby and let me know where she leads you."

"I got you, boo." He disconnects the call.

"Ticky, I'm going to call a few of my killas you call a few of yours. Tell them to be on standby. As soon as this bitch leads Tokyo to these niggas, we going to knock they ass off like wind to a loose wig."

"Say less, my nigga."

Paris was a nervous wreck and her worries were at an all-time high as she flew down the highway chain-smoking a box of Newport cigarette. After a barrage of calls to Baby Red with no answer, she activated the tracking device on his phone. The tracker led her out of the city to Madison. Which scared her that much more. Baby Red didn't mess around in Madison. Because judges in Madison handed out harsher sentences than the ones in Milwaukee when it came to dope cases. He had learned that lesson from a few of his homeboys that had gone out there to get money. When ounces of dope were going for nine hundred in Milwaukee, cats in the Madison area was paying close to eleven. That brought a lot of hustlers out there to fall for the judicial trap. Because of that, Baby Red stayed away from Madison on that tip. Knowing this she couldn't help but wonder if somebody, maybe the men that just robbed their house, did something to him. Maybe they kidnapped him and beat him until he told them where to find the dope. Maybe killed him and then came to rob the house. She didn't know what to think. Her mind was everywhere. All she knew it wasn't like Baby Red to ignore her calls. Something had to be wrong. Not knowing what to expect when she got to where the tracking device lead her, she grabbed Wee Wee and Do-Dirty to ride with her.

"Wee Wee, I'm telling you something just don't feel right. This ain't like Red."

"Just calm down cuz. We gon find him and if anybody has laid a hand on him, we gon kill they ass."

"You say them niggas took all the work?"

"Fuck that dope right now, Do-Dirty! My man, yo cousin is missing. This ain't the time to worry about no goddamn drugs!"

"I hear you, but shit. Billy Gunz, or whatever his name is, gets out this week. Baby Red said his self if that man's dope or money ain't there when he gets out, all hell is gonna break loose."

"Like I said, we'll worry about that after we find Baby Red." Even though he just added more worries to her already over-worried mind. She knew Do-Dirty was right. But right now, she only wanted to focus on finding Baby Red.

***

He stretches in the bed as he awakens from a night of much-needed sleep. "What that clock say, baby?" he asks Classy who laid on his chest watching TV.

117

"It is…" She reaches behind her and grabs her cellphone off the nightstand. "9:30 on the dot." Baby Red jumps out of bed.

"Shit! Why you let me sleep so long?" He hurries into the bathroom and gets into the shower.

"You needed your rest baby. You wouldn't be any good in these streets if you didn't get it!" she yells to him from the bed as she rolled a blunt. Several minutes later while watching one of her favorite reality shows, a knock came at the door. She gets up and answers the door. When she opens the door, she's quickly pushed back in at gunpoint as Do-Dirty, Wee Wee and Paris ran in. Once inside, Wee Wee is able to get a good look at her and when he saw that fat ass on her he knew then exactly who she was and the real reason why Baby Red wasn't answering the phone. But it was nothing he could do to cover for him. It was too late; Paris was there and could see what's going on for herself. Classy stood there in her bra and panties with her hands up. The bathroom door opens, and he yells, "Baby, spark that blunt up for me." Not being any wiser to what's going on, out walks Baby Red with a towel wrapped around his waist. "Ah, shit! Paris, baby."

"If you give me that corny ass line about it's not what it looks like, I'm going to kill you myself. I'm going to deal with you in a second. Right now, I got a bitch's ass to beat." Paris rushed Classy hitting her in the face. Classy swings back catching Paris on the side of the head. They grab each other by the hair and exchange blows before falling over on the bed. They wrestle for a minute and fall out the bed knocking the lamp to the floor causing it to shatter. After getting his clothes on, Baby Red tries to break it up. But trying to pull the two women apart proved to be more of a challenge than he thought. Every time he pulls one apart, the other one rushes.

"Y'all want to quit standing there and give me some help!"

"Not really. This shit is entertaining," Do-Dirty says.

"Like some straight Jerry Springer type shit," Wee Wee adds in.

"Get y'all ass over here and help!" Wee Wee and Do-Dirty grab Classy and pull her back.

"Control your bitch, Baby Red. I can't believe this the type of trash you have been putting up with!"

"Bitch, you the trash!"

"Come back to Atlanta with me. It's obvious it's too much negativity here for you." Paris breaks loose from his grasp and turns around to face him.

"So, this is what you doing down in Atlanta? Humping around town with this bitch?" Baby Red couldn't say anything. "While I'm at home with guns to my head, you over here getting your dick wet with this trailer tramp!" Baby Red's heart sunk.

"What you mean you had a gun to your head? You okay?" he asks with pain and anger in his heart that somebody dared put a gun to the head of the woman he loved more than anything in the world.

"I'm standing here, ain't I? But they made away with the work."

"WHAT! No, no this is not happening, This is not fucking happening! Billy Gunz will be out this week. What the fuck is I'm supposed to do now?"

"Like I said, baby, come back to Atlanta and you won't have to worry about all this bullshit."

"I'm going to kill this bitch," Paris says, trying to run up on her, but Baby Red holds her back. "Red, you better tell this bitch right now what it is, or I'm gone!"

"Yea, tell her who you choose, so you can be done with all this unnecessary drama and we can go back to Georgia where we can live in peace."

"I don't know what you thought, but I would never leave my wifey for another bitch. No matter how good that head and pussy is." Classy snatches free from Do-Dirty and Wee Wee.

"You going to choose this bitch over me? I'm the one who put you on in Atlanta, Baby Red. I'm the one who takes FED risks to get your dope down there! And this is how you repay me? You quit me?" she says, putting her clothes on and gathering her things.

"It was fun while it lasted."

"Go to hell," she says pushing past to the door. She opens it and sees a bunch of men come rushing towards the room with guns. She couldn't say a word, she couldn't even move. Like a deer in the headlights, all she could do was stand there in shock and hope her death came quick so she wouldn't feel any pain.

~ CHAPTER 15 ~

"I followed her to the Regency Motel over here on the West Side of Madison. And just like I thought, babe, all the birds are in the same nest. Baby Red's Charger is parked right outside. They're in room 113... Alright, see you when you get here." Tokyo hangs up the phone. She was more than happy to help Truth locate Baby Red. It was nothing more she would like to see than his body riddled with bullets. And to her, it would be quite the bonus to see Paris get hers in the midst. Baby Red could never know the type of enemy he made with Tokyo when he cheated on her with Paris. To find out he was having an affair with the one woman in the club that she considered a friend and confided in, shattered her heart to pieces. Pieces that even now that she's with Truth, she still hasn't been able to put back together. She only got with Truth because he's Baby Red's competition. She knew it would kill him to see them together. She wanted him to stew in the pain of how she felt. Even though eventually her and Truth's bond grew, due to their mutual hate for Baby Red, her need for revenge wasn't satisfied. She now wanted his ass dead right along with Paris. She couldn't help not letting an evil smile take over her face as she thought how tonight she'll be getting just what she's been praying for. Both Baby Red and Paris in a box.

Seeing her eyes grow wide when she opened the door, Wee Wee's instincts kicked in. He pulled his pistol and ran to the door pushing Classy to the floor, knocking off two shots at the men that were rushing their way towards them. He slammed the door close and locked it. Do-Dirty, on point with him, pushed the long hotel dresser in front of the door. Baby Red grabs his gun and cocks it back and loading one in the chamber. Paris pulls out the Glock 40 she brought from home

121

and cocks it back. She takes cover behind the bed with Wee Wee and Baby Red. Classy crawled to the bathroom and took cover in the bathtub. Do-Dirty crouched down in the doorway of the bathroom just before the bullets began flying all across the room. Baby Red fires two shots at the door. "Wee Wee, how many did you see?"

"I don't know, a lot!" AK-47 bullets riddled the hotel walls making them all duck back down. "I know one thing, we ain't got enough ammo to shoot it out with all them niggas out there."

"Red, what are we going to do!" Paris asks, ducking down as bullets and debris fly past her. The men outside were trying to kick the door in while others sent shots through the wall to keep Baby Red and em from firing back at the door. Baby Red looks around the room trying to find a way out.

"Over there! Dirt kick in that door that leads to the room next door. Me and Wee Wee will cover you." Do-Dirty nods his head and opens the door on their end of the room then began kicking in the adjoining door. It wasn't giving him any signs of coming open. He kicked hard as he could, but the door wouldn't budge. "Dirt hurry up!"

"Fuck this." Do-Dirty pointed his gun at the door lock and shot the door open. "Come on!" Paris crawls into the other room. Do-Dirty grabs a pillow and puts the gun to it to suppress its sound. That way the men outside wouldn't hear him shooting the locks off on the door in the next room. Classy stayed balled up in the bathtub crying and screaming as the bullets flew passed

"Classy, let's go!"

"I can't. I'm scared!"

So much for that Grady's Holmes projects, down ass, ride or die chick shit she was talking earlier, Baby Red thought to himself. He crawled over to her and yanked her out the tub.

"Bitch, get yo ass out the tub, and let's go!" She crawled behind him sobbing. The dresser started to move as the room door began to open. Wee Wee sends two shots at the door and the sounds of a man grunting and falling to the floor let him know he hit his target. They make their way to the next room where a prostitute and her client sat huddled up in bed terrified and holding on to each other. Do-Dirty leads them all through two more rooms before peeping out the front door of the last one. Seeing the coast was clear, they made their way outside.

Crouched down beside a U-Haul truck, Baby Red checks his magazine clip then slips it back in. He peeps out from behind the truck to get the layout of the parking lot and see how many they were up against. "What it look like out there, Baby Red?"

"This nigga brought a squad with him, Dirt. I counted six in the parking lot alone, plus Truth and Ticky. That's not even including the niggas that's inside searching the motel rooms for us."

"Yea, it won't be long before they realize we made it outside already. So, we better get moving."

"With all the gunshots I'm sure the manager or someone notified the cops by now. Can't we just hide somewhere 'til they show up?" Paris rolls her eyes at Classy's question.

"How about you go hide, you dumb bitch? Watch how they tear this whole motel up until they find and kill every last one of us before the police even get here."

"What's the plan, Baby Red?" Wee Wee asks. Baby Red takes another peek from behind the truck. Truth and Ticky pretty much had the parking lot surrounded. The motel stretched around into the shape of the letter U. In the center of the motel was a six-row parking lot with twenty cars per row. Thanks to the lack of available front row parking spots, none of their cars were nearby. He spots Paris's car three rows back and three cars to the left of their current position. Baby Red's car was parked in the second row four cars to the left of them. Classy's car was parked in the third row behind the set of cars that were parked directly in front of them. He knew he could get everybody to their cars. But because of the parking lot's U shape, it had only one way in and one way out, and Ticky and Truth had the exit covered. Not to mention Truth's Benz was parked sideways, in no particular parking spot, right in front of were Baby Red's car was parked. Truth and Ticky stood outside of Truth's car along with one their goons posted by the front bumper of Baby Red's car. Two more goons stood on each side of the doorway of the room. Another one stood four doors to the left of the room and the remaining two stood near a van in the center of the parking lot.

Baby Red thinks fast and comes up with a plan after giving them the layout of Truth, Ticky, and their goon's positions.

"Baby, you still got the extra alarm pad to my car on your keyring?"

"Yea, it's right here," she says pulling it out her pocket.

"Okay. When you make it to your car, I want you to hit the panic button on my alarm. And when y'all hear us start busting, I want both you to get in y'all cars and get the hell out of here as fast y'all can."

"But you said they have the exit covered," Classy says.

"Don't worry about that, me and fellas will keep them busy." Baby Red peeps out from the back of the truck. He sees an opening and waves Paris and Classy off. Like mice sneaking around a well-lit kitchen, they quickly crept to the next row of cars. Classy makes it to her car first and stays crouched down by its driver's door awaiting the signal. Baby Red turns to Wee Wee and Do-Dirty. "When Paris gives the signal, we going to fan out. Wee Wee, remember it's two men next to that van in the third row. They stand in the way of both Paris and Classy getting out of here. I want you to go that way and take care of them. Dirt, I want you to stay here and cover me. I'm going to move Truth and Ticky around so the girls can make their exit. Once they do, everybody needs to make their way to my car. Understood?" They both nod their heads in agreement.

"You think this is gonna work?" Wee Wee asks.

"Just cross your fingers and send up a quick prayer that it does. Start busting and hope like hell that we all make it out of here alive."

Paris makes it to her car. She takes a deep breath. "Here goes nothing." She presses the button and the panic alarm on Baby Red's Charger goes off. All the gunmen follow their natural reaction and turned their attention and guns towards the source of the noise, giving Baby Red and em that split-second distraction they needed to catch them off guard.

Baby Red comes out from the front of the U-Haul truck busting at the men that stood outside the room door, giving them doom shots causing them to fall dead instantly. Wee Wee came out from the tail end of the truck making his way to the third row while Do-Dirty covered him. He caught the attention of the men near the van and they exchange gunfire. Wee Wee ran down to the fifth row making the men follow.

Seeing she was in the clear, Classy hops in her car starts it up, and smashes out. Truth and Ticky jump out the way of her speeding car as it flew past. Before they could aim their guns, she was already out of the parking lot.

Paris stays low opening her car door, but before she could even get in, the sound of a gun cocking came from behind her.

"And where you think you're going, bitch?" Tokyo says holding the gun to the back of Paris's head.

Do-Dirty fired a shot that almost hit Truth in the side making him take cover. Two men came out of the motel room that

Baby Red and em made their exit out of. They catch Do-Dirty off guard and started firing shots at him. One shot hit him in the shoulder. He quickly empties his clip on the em, dropping them in the doorway. He crawls over and picks up their guns and makes his way closer to Baby Red's car.

Baby Red picks up a chopper one of the goons that he dropped was carrying. He spits shots at Truth and Ticky pinning them in beside a tan old school Cutlass.

Wee Wee knocked one of the shooters off, but still had another one on his heels spitting at him with a Tec. Wee Wee took cover behind a green Suburban truck. The man sprays shots in his direction. One of the bullets flies past Tokyo and goes through Paris's back passenger's window. The shot made Tokyo duck down and let out a brief scream. It gave Paris enough time to turn around with a gun already in hand and pop a shot straight to her head. Tokyo's brains sprayed out onto the window of the car behind her and her body hit the ground. Paris hops in the car and smashed out of the parking space. The man shooting at Wee Wee stood in the middle of the lane shooting and didn't see Paris speeding behind him. She hit him hard causing his body to fly ten feet in the air and land headfirst on the pavement shattering his skull.

Paris didn't stop, she sped towards the exit like Baby Red told her to. Ticky and Truth concentrate their guns on her as she came their way. Baby Red sends shots from the Ak-47 at them to redirect their attention. Paris squeezed the steering wheel tight and put the gas pedal to the floor as she flew to the exit. She flies out the parking lot turning right and almost flipping the car over, but gains control and were gone.

Wee Wee ducks down behind Baby Red's car and awaits the others. Do-Dirty, four cars away from Wee Wee, blasts at Truth and Ticky while Baby Red shoots at them from another angle. Baby Red sees Wee Wee made to the car. "Wee Wee, get us going, baby." He throws the keys across the parking lot to him. The keys land near the front bumper. He crawls over and gets them. Then jumps in and starts the car up. Do-Dirty makes it over towards the car as Wee Wee pulls out of the parking space.

"Baby Red, let's ride!" Do-Dirty covers Baby Red as he shoots his way over to the car.

They get in and peel out the parking lot and was in the wind before Ticky and Truth could get in their car and follow.

***

"Pull over there behind that white Cadillac." The second man that participated in the home invasion on Baby Red's house tell the lead man. They get out the car and the second man preceded to take the duffle bag of dope out of the getaway car and load it into the trunk of the Cadillac.

"Ooh wee! We in the money now! I can't wait to get my cut home. I finna throw a primo party," the lead man says.

"What the fuck is a primo party?"

"It's a party where I invite all my smoker friends over and we get high all-night smoking weed laced with dope." The second man shakes his head at him and closes the trunk. The lead man looks down at the trunk with a look of confusion and he clears his throat.

"You know I'm leaving in my Impala right here, right?"

"I know."

"So, my cut?"

"Oh, yea about that." The second man pulls out a gun and pops him in the head. He gets in the passenger seat of the Cadillac and the driver pulls off.

~ CHAPTER 16 ~

Baby Red just received the phone call he been dreading. Billy Gunz called letting him know he was out and that he wanted to meet with him tomorrow.

But all news wasn't bad news. Instead of the niggas who broke into the house making it away with twenty-one bricks, they only made away with eleven. While Baby Red was taking his safety measures, Paris took hers. Besides installing the tracking device on his phone, she split the bricks up. She only kept so many at the house and stashed the rest in a storage unit on the other side of town.

Baby Red and his team sat at the table counting up the money and dope they had left for Billy Gunz. "What is it looking like, baby?" Paris does a final calculation before responding.

"Okay, if we subtract the ten zips you get off every key that would put us at owing Billy Gunz 286 ounces. But when we subtract your ten ounces off each of the ten keys that we have left, we end up owing him 178 ounces. Roughly a little over five keys. And at 17.5 a brick that means we owe him $87,500.00."

"Damn!" Baby Red says, slamming his fist on the table.

"So not only do we give him everything we got, leaving us all broke as hell. You're saying that we'll still be in the hole with this nigga?" Do-Dirty says from across the table with his left arm in a sling.

"Yup," Paris says double-checking the numbers.

"What about the four bricks we brought down south? We still got a lil over three left," Noodles says.

"It wouldn't matter. We would still owe him, and we still wouldn't be able to cop shit. And you know Billy Gunz ain't finna front Baby Red shit with this war going on," Pay Pay answers her.

"I say we hit that Mexican bitch you were telling us about in Atlanta. Catch her coming out of the church and make off with that diaper bag," Wee Wee suggests, while dumping his blunt ashes into the ashtray.

"Your suggestion is that we rob a whale to pay a shark?" Pay Pay asks him. Wee Wee shrugs his shoulders.

"With all the bricks Billy Gunz be buying at once, it should be enough money in there to pay him off and re-up on our own," he replies.

"Let that be a very last resort," Baby Red tells him.

"So, what we gon do? Your meeting with Billy Gunz is tomorrow," Pay Pay asks him.

"I'm going to holla at him and see if I can buy us some time while I further figure things out."

"Don't forget we still got other problems at hand. Ticky and Truth. And Truth is beyond pissed behind Tokyo's death."

"I know, Noodles. That's why we gonna go at these niggas hard. Get rid of their asses once and for all, so we can go back to business as usual. Once this war is over, Billy Gunz should have no problems fronting us again. In the meantime, everybody keep yo heat close and remain low key."

Baby Red pulls up to Dean Park. He gets out of the car and scans the park for Billy Gunz and spots him at the chess table area. A call comes into his phone. "Hello."

"Take a seat at the empty chess table to the right of him. Don't look in his direction, act like you don't know him, and keep the conversation cryptic," Missy says then disconnects the call.

He walks over and does what he was told. Billy Gunz played a game of chess with a mixed breed teenage boy. Billy Gunz takes the boy's rook on 41 with his bishop on 6. The boy takes Billy Gunz's bishop on 41 with his bishop on 59. An old man walks over to Baby Red's table. "Mind if I play a game with you, son?" Without looking his direction, Billy Gunz nods his head giving Baby Red the okay. Baby Red and the old man began setting up their pieces.

Billy Gunz takes his opponent's bishop with his pawn on 34. The boy creeps his knight on 58, closer to Billy Gunz's queen on 31.

"You look a lil stress there, Baby Red."

"I'm alright."

"This level of the game ain't as easy as you thought it would be, huh?"

"It has its struggle. Ain't nothing I can't handle."

"Is that right? I went to mass yesterday when I came home. And when I spoke with the priest, he told me you haven't been in for your weekly confession. You must want to put an end to your blessings and piss God off."

"Not at all. I just ran into some problems."

"This wouldn't have nothing to do with this war I've been hearing about, would it?" Baby Red didn't have a response for him. "Listen here, Baby Red, your problems ain't my problem. And if they were to ever become my problem, then I promise you are not going to like the solution."

"I got this."

"No, you got seven days to have it. And not a day later." Billy's opponent smiled as he moved his Knight on 37 to 31 finally taking possession of Billy Gunz's queen.

"Got yo bitch," the boy says with triumph. Billy Gunz shakes his head as he looks down at the board.

"Some king you are. Look at you, you done sacrifice your whole kingdom for a bitch," he tells his opponent as he moves his pawn from 43 to 51, and with another pawn on 42 protecting it, he checkmates him. "Seven days, Baby Red, and the clock is ticking," he tells him, then gets up dust his hands off, and leaves.

***

His face was ravished with pain as he watched them lower Tokyo's casket into the ground. He hadn't slept in days and vowed to not sleep until Baby Red was dead.

He couldn't get the image out his head. The image of Tokyo's soulless body lying face down on the pavement with her brains oozing out of the back of her head. Ticky had to pry him away from her as the sound of the police sirens became closer.

He kisses a pink rose and throws it on top of her casket. It was her favorite rose and when she was alive, he bought her dozens of them at the beginning of each month. He walks off with Ticky by his side. "I'm tired of this nigga slipping away from us, Ticky. Fuck these sloppy ass goons, I'm going to handle this myself. This shit has gotten even more personal now." They hop into the black limo that awaited them.

"I know what you mean. And right now, them niggas is in hiding. I've been combing these streets heavy for their ass. But trust and believe that worm ass nigga, Do-Dirty, and Baby Red's bitch ass ain't gon be able to hide from us for long. I got something to bring their asses out."

"What you have in mind?"

"I'll tell you in a second." Ticky pulls out his phone and dials Dee Dee. "Dee Dee, Terry at the house?"

"Yea."

"Put her on the phone."

"She sleep!"

"Bitch, wake her up!" She smacks her lips.

"Hold on." A few seconds go by and then Terry answers the phone with a groggy voice.

"Hello?"

"Terry, you get that info for me?" Terry yawns on the other end of the phone.

"Yea, I got it Ticky. It wasn't easy though. None of the smokers around here knew where to find them. But another hype buddy of mine from the South Side told me about some bomb ass dope that was going around over there. He took me to a dope spot on 15th and Washington across the street from McDonald's. And sure enough, that's where Baby Red and em are hiding out. Now, can I go back to sleep Ticky? I've been up all night getting high."

"Good looking out baby girl. I'm gonna take care of you when I get home. Gon get some sleep."

Ticky disconnects the call and turns his attention to Truth. "We now know where they're hiding out at, so let's go end this shit."

***

Pay Pay and Noodles sat in the drive-thru of Krystal's fast food restaurant. It was one of the hottest summer days in Georgia and Noodles was getting irritated as they waited in the long line of cars to place their order. She turns the AC on full blast and points the vent her way. "Go Pay Pay!" Pay Pay was checking something on his phone and didn't see the line had moved.

"My bad."

"Out of all the restaurants in Atlanta, I don't know why you had to pick this crowded ass restaurant to go to."

"Relax. I'm telling you, Noodles. You're going to love this joint, baby. It's just like White Castle. And we both know how much you love White Castle burgers."

"Yea whatever. You talked to the crew?"

"I was just texting Baby Red back. He had hit me up letting me know how the meeting went with Billy Gunz."

"And how he say it went?"

"He said Billy Gunz gave him a week to come up with all the money."

"I'm so done with this shit." Pay Pay pulls up to the intercom and places their order then rolls the window back up.

"What you mean by that?"

"Meaning I'm done, I'm out!"

"What you saying, just going to abandon the crew like that?"

"Do-Dirty and Baby Red both are going to end up getting us killed with their stupidity. I love Baby Red and em like they were my own brothers, but you got to admit, Pay Pay, Baby Red has been making some reckless decisions. And now we got all this drama going on back in the Mil because of those decisions.

You know something when we're here in Atlanta, I'm at peace. We hustle, we get our money, and don't have to worry about anything. But when we go back to the Mil, it's nothing but stress.

I used to love my city, Pay Pay, but now I dread every time we have to go back there. It's like when we are there, I can't wait to leave and when we are here, I never want to go. I just can't do it anymore." He pulls up to the window and pays for their food. The man hands him their food and drinks. Pay Pay passes it to Noodles to hold.

"This coming from the woman who used to get geeked up when it was time to bust them guns. What happen baby? Shit got too real for you?"

"I just have things that are way more important to be concern about."

"Like what?" he aska as he reaches over into the bag on her lap and pulls out a hand full of fries. The smell of the food made her feel nauseous. She couldn't hold her stomach any longer. She tosses the food to him then quickly opens the door and starts vomiting.

"Like the fact that I'm pregnant," she says wiping her mouth and closing the door. A horn blow behind them and Pay Pay pulls off.

Shock had gripped him, and his mind began to race. He couldn't believe it and yet all the signs were there. The weird cravings for pizza with ranch sauce and Flaming Hot Cheeto's on top, the frequent trips to the bathroom, and the mood swings, all the signs he missed.

"I'm keeping the baby, and you ain't got to worry about feeling obligated to take care of it either. I have no problem doing it on my own," she says interrupting his thoughts.

"What? What kind of nigga you take me for? I'm not letting you raise our child by yourself."

"And I'm not going to put our child at risk by being caught up in that mess back in Wisconsin!" Silence invaded the truck for several moments as Pay Pay gathered his thoughts. He takes a turn off their normal route to their motel. "You turned off too early Pay Pay. You supposed had kept straight for five more blocks before turning."

"We're not going to the motel just yet."

"Then where we going? Because I'm tired and it's too damn hot for any extra activities. I need to go lay my ass down."

He pulls up in front of a small brick single-family house with a rent to own sign out front.

"If you're done with Wisconsin and the crew, then I'm done too. And if we're going to be here, we might as well make it home," he says pointing to the house.

~ CHAPTER 17 ~

"Let's get this straight, Amanda. You say you weren't at the motel, yet the room is in your name and the woman at the front desk says she could swear to it that you were the one who rented the room," Detective Hicks tells her.

"No n-no that's not what I said. Yea, I rented the room, but I wasn't there when all the shooting was going on." Classy starts to get nervous. She thought when she made it out of the parking lot and back to Atlanta, she left Baby Red and everything that happened in Wisconsin in her rearview. When the detectives showed up at her house this morning asking her to come down to the station for questioning, she nearly fainted. The detectives had run the name on the motel room. and came back with her address in Atlanta. They were on the next flight there questioning her.

"It was your room door that was kicked in and it looked as if someone had moved the dresser to barricade the door maybe. If you say you weren't there, and they weren't shooting at you, then who were they shooting at? That's a lot of rounds shot off to be shooting at no one, Ms. Nelson. Don't you think?"

"Maybe they had the wrong room. Or maybe they were shooting at the man you found dead in front of the room door. I'm telling you that I wasn't there! I don't know what happened!"

"I call bullshit," Detective Marks walks in the room and says. Then tosses a stack of photos on the table in front of Classy.

"What's this?" she says before looking down at the photos in front of her.

"Those are still shots of your car and plate number captured from a traffic cam a block away from the motel. It seems you must've been in quite the hurry to have run a red light.

And if you look closely at the little timer at the bottom there, it says this was at 10:26 PM. That's around the same time of the shooting."

"And another thing Ms. Nelson, I never told you anyone was found dead in front of the room door. That information wasn't even given to the press. Only someone who was present at the time of the shooting could've known that bit of information," Detective Hicks says, snd takes a slow sip of his coffee without taking his eyes off her.

Beads of sweat began to form on the back of her neck and her hands and legs start to tremble. Detective Marks sees she's close to folding so he applies more pressure.

"Ms. Nelson, as you know, a lot of people were killed at that motel. For right now, the only suspect we have is you."

"Suspect? But I didn't kill anyone."

"Maybe not. But I have to tell you that's not the way the courts will see it. All the evidence we have points to you. It was your room and your car speeding away from the scene of the crime." He looks to Detective Hicks. "How much time they're giving out these days for first-degree murder in Wisconsin?"

"Life."

"And you can multiply that by seven. Meaning you will never see the light of day again."

The idea of possibly spending the rest of her life in prison shook her to her very core. Classy feels her heart pounding so hard she expected that at any moment it was going to jump right out her chest. The air in the room became very dry to her making it hard for her to swallow.

Classy starts breaking down and crying. Detective Hicks moves in for the kill. "Amanda, I know you are a good person. I know you weren't the one who did this. You were just at the wrong place at the wrong time with the wrong crowd. Am I right?" Between her sobs, she shakes her head yes. He gives her a cigarette and lights it for her "Then tell us what really happen?"

Classy has never been a gangsta, but she has never been a snitch either. She hated snitches. A snitch is something she always said wasn't in her to be. But with the pressure on her, she became the very person she hated and never in a million years thought she would be. And just like that, Classy began to tell the detectives everything.

"Okay dig this Ernie, if you can eat this whole pack of saltine crackers in less than a minute, I'll give you this rock, for free." Wee Wee holds up a fat rock for Ernie to see.

"Come wit it."

"Hold on now. Hear the whole deal first. You can't drink anything until you chewed and swallowed every last cracker. And if you can't do it within sixty seconds, then you have to wash my car for a week."

"Wee Wee, stop being childish and taking advantage of Ernie's slow ass. Everybody with at least half brain knows damn well it's physically impossible to eat a whole pack of saltine crackers in less than a minute without water," Paris says. Wee Wee waves her off.

"Man, you down or what?"

"Let's do this." Wee Wee sets the timer on his phone.

"Ready...Go!" Ernie takes the open pack of crackers and begins stuffing them in his mouth. He finds it to be a lot harder than he expected. As he chewed the crackers, they began to absorb all the moisture in his mouth. He swallows half of what's in his mouth and stuffs some more in. "You got thirty seconds left, big dog." With still less than half a pack left Ernie tries to chew faster. But he couldn't swallow it his mouth was too dry. "Ten...nine...eight...seven..." Ernie tried swallowing again and choked so hard that he shitted on himself as he coughed up the crackers.

"Ugh, uh uh, get his stanking ass up out of here," Paris says holding her nose. Wee Wee gives him the bag of dope anyway and pushes him out the door.

"You still gon be washing my car next week!" He closes the door and takes a seat on the couch next to Do-Dirty. Seconds later, Baby Red walks into the house with a bag. He pours the contents of the bag out on the table. Racks of money and a kilo and a half of dope fall out. He plops down on the couch and buries his face in his hand.

"What's wrong, baby?" Paris comes over with a blunt and takes a seat on his lap.

"Pay Pay and Noodles just left."

"Why they didn't come in and say what's up?"

"This wasn't no social visit. They brought back all the dope and money they had. They say they're out. They say they're staying in Atlanta and don't plan on coming back up here again."

"That bitch and bitch ass nigga, man. How they just gon up and call it a quits when we in the middle of a war? That's what I be saying about these disloyal ass mothafuckas. After we lay down Truth and Ticky and take our dope back, we should go off they ass too," Do-Dirty says.

"I don't blame them. All this is been too much for anyone to deal with. You ask me, they got the right idea about getting the hell out of here. I think we all should take notes from their book and do the same. We got three days left to have this man's money. I say instead of paying Billy Gunz back and being broke, we should just split everything up three ways and get the hell out of dodge."

"And go where?" Baby Red looks at her and asks.

"Las Vegas, New York, California, anywhere but here!"

"I'm all for splitting the money and dope up. But ain't feeling that leaving nonsense. This my city and I ain't leaving this bitch for nothing or nobody." Do-Dirty says.

"It's something seriously mentally wrong with you. You actually think Billy Gunz would let you live knowing you owe him?"

"Baby Red owes him, not me."

"Boom, there it is. I told you that Do-Dirty didn't give a damn about nobody but himself," Paris says, pointing her finger at him and looking at Baby Red.

"Nigga, you actually fixed yo mouth to say something like that? When the only reason we're all in this mess is because of you!"

"That ain't how I meant it. What I'm saying is Billy Gunz don't know me and I don't know him. So, there's no reason he would be looking for me."

"That don't sound no less self-centered. What about me, Paris and Wee Wee? He knows us." Do-Dirty shrugs his shoulders.

"Y'all talking about leaving town, then leave town. You go far enough, he won't be able to find you."

"And what about Ticky and Truth?"

"You said we finna go deal with them, right? What, now that y'all talking about leaving town, we ain't trying to get the bricks back anymore?"

"First off, I didn't agree with leaving town or dividing the money. I'm still pursuing our original plan of getting the birds back from Truth and Ticky and paying Billy Gunz back before the clocks up."

"Man, how we even know it's them that got our shit? You just said yesterday, Do-Dirty, yo clucks been hitting up yo line. You said they have been begging you to come through cause the dope on that end is garbage. So, if he and Ticky ain't popping them bricks off on their turf, why should we believe they even got em?" Wee Wee adds in while he polishes his Draco.

"Make sense. But who else could have them?"

"Both of y'all tripping. It can't be anybody but Truth and Ticky that took them bricks. They probably pushing them somewhere else or holding on to them until the heat dies down. So, let's stick to the plan of going to get our shit. And when we get it, we do like Paris suggested and divide everything up. Fuck Billy Gunz." The doorbell rings.

"I'll get it!" Linda says, coming out the back room.

"Make sure you see who it is first before you open that door," Do-Dirty tells her.

"You ain't got to tell me, I know better," she says, walking past the living room and into the entrance hall that lead to the front door. "Who is it?" She looks through the peephole.

"It's Pickles!" the woman on the other side of the door replies.

"It's just my homegirl Pickles y'all." As soon as the door opens, *BOOM!* A bullet pierces Pickle's skull, splattering her brains all over Linda's face. Before Linda had time to react, *BOOM!* A second shot goes off, hitting her in the eye dropping her to the floor instantly. Ticky steps to the side and Truth walks up with an M-16 and starts spraying as he walked through the doorway.

The entrance hall was to the front and closer to the left side of the room. There was a door leading to a bedroom on the right side of the living room. Do-Dirty took cover in its doorway and bust back. The couch that Baby Red and Paris sat on faced the entrance hall. The entrance to the kitchen sat to the right of the couch. When the first shot went off, Paris and Baby Red scrammed to the kitchen with guns in hand. Wee

Wee quickly loads the clip back into the Draco and start busting back as he made his way to the kitchen.

Truth and Ticky take cover in the entrance hall as Wee Wee and Do-Dirty pins them in. "You a dead man, Baby Red!" Truth yells to him.

"Then why I'm still breathing?" he yells back from the kitchen. Paris tries to get to the back door to remove the three 2x4 boards that enforced the door, but the steady shots flying past brought much hindrance to her mission.

"Baby Red do something! I can't get to the door with them shooting at me!" Paris tells him.

"I got you, baby! Hold tight!" He bust two shots from the kitchen then yells to Wee Wee and Do-Dirty. "Dirt, Wee Wee, let's spray these roaches up out of here!" He then rushes out the kitchen busting before taking cover behind the couch next to Wee Wee. Truth unleashes his whole clip wildly making them all duck down. As he tries to reload a fresh clip, the crew sends a parade of shots that forced them out the door. Baby Red and Do-Dirty run after them busting, while Wee Wee grabs his new toy.

"I've been waiting to try this mothafucka out," he says, grabbing an old school Tommy gun and running out the front door.

The gunfight spills out into the streets. Do-Dirty pop off three shots from behind a tree. One of the shots catches Ticky in the leg and knocks him over. Do-Dirty smiled and got ready to rush over and finish him off, but Truth sends shots that kept him pinned behind the tree. "Ticky, you good?" Ticky groans as he gets back to his feet.

"Yea, that bitch got me in the leg!"

"Can you get to the car?"

"Yea!"

"I'll cover you!" Ticky hops as fast as he could to the McDonald's parking lot. Truth bust, giving them both cover. Wee Wee lets the old school typewriter loose. Two shots hit Truth in the shoulder and thigh. Truth stumbled but remained unfazed as he kept busting and making their way to the car.

"I'm going to make sure Paris got out. Keep pushing these niggas back," Baby Red says before running back into the house yelling for Paris. He makes his way towards the kitchen hoping she left out the back door already. But she didn't. One board remained on the door and Paris laid on the floor in a pool of blood. "No, no, nooo!" Her eyes were closed and her breathing shallow. He scooped her up quickly.

"I like this bitch!" Wee Wee says admiring the spit of the Tommy gun, but his moment of admiration was short-lived as Ticky bust three shots off hitting Wee Wee in the chest.

"Wee Wee!" Do-Dirty yells busting his way towards Wee Wee's body. He sees it's nothing he could do. Wee Wee was already gone. One bullet pierced his heart killing him instantly.

Baby Red comes rushing out the door with Paris cradled in his arms. "Dirt, we got to go!" Do-Dirty covers him as Baby Red gets in the backseat with Paris. Do-Dirty jumps and the driver's seat and smashes off with bullets bouncing off the car just as several squad cars began pulling up.

"Truth, let's go!" Ticky yelled from the car. Truth seed their chances of getting away together was slimmed to none.

"You get up out of here, dog, while I take care of these fleas on yo ass."

"You sure you want to go out like this?"

"Yup!" He loaded a fresh clip and started busting as the police came. Ticky peeled out.

~ CHAPTER 18 ~

Blood poured from the two gunshot wounds in her back and side. Baby Red uses the shirt off his back to try and stop the bleeding. She was still unconscious and barely breathing. Do-Dirty whipped the Charger in and out of traffic. "Dirt! Hurry up and get us to that damn hospital!"

"We almost there, cuz."

Do-Dirty comes flying into the hospital parking lot with the car horn blaring. He brings the Charger's tires screaming to a stop behind an ambulance in front of the emergency entrance. They hop out of the car. "We need some help over here!" Baby Red yells as the ambulance drivers come rushing over. Seconds later, nurses rush out with a stretcher.

"We have a pulse! It's very faint! Let's get her to the operating room now!" one of the nurses yell and they rush Paris through the emergency doors. Baby Red follows behind them. When they get to the doors of the operating room, the nurse stops him. "Sir please, you have to wait in the waiting room."

"That's my girl in there. I'm not leaving her side."

"Please, let us do what we do. I promise you, she's in good hands and we're going to do all we can for her." Baby Red reluctantly stepped down and the nurse ran into the room to attend to Paris.

He paced the floor in the waiting room. Do-Dirty walked over to him. "Yo, we got to roll."

"I can't leave Paris."

"You ain't got a choice." Do-Dirty points over at the nurses' station. "The police are here and they gonna have a lot of questions to ask. And we got way too many guns in the car right now to answer them." Baby Red looks over and sees the nurse talking to the cops and pointing in their direction. The police leave the nurse's station and move towards them. Baby Red starts walking off.

"Excuse me, sir!" the police say from behind them. They walk faster towards the exit. "Sir!" As they get to the front door, one of the doctors tries to block their exit. Do-Dirty swings off, busting him in the nose. The doctor falls to the floor with his nose flowing blood between his fingers. They run to the car as the police officers start giving chase behind them, but Baby Red and Do-Dirty had too much distance on them. They hop in and Do-Dirty smashes off.

***

"She made it out of surgery, but she slipped into a coma. The doctors say all we can do now is pray," Shirley, Paris mama tells Baby Red over the phone.

"Alright Shirley, keep me updated if her condition changes."

"I will, but before you go, I got to let you know the FEDs are looking for you."

"Why the FEDs?" Baby Red could see the police questioning him about the shooting. But the FEDs? That brought his worries to a whole new level.

"Yea. Word is an informant told the FEDs about a drug business you've been running between Georgia and Wisconsin." His heart sank to the pit of his stomach.

"Alright, I'ma talk to you later. Good looking out. Hit me back if you hear something new."

"Will do." He disconnects the phone. He wondered who could've ratted him out to the FEDs. His suspicion made Pay Pay, Noodles, and Classy all suspects.

Baby Red pays his admission fee into the Milwaukee County Zoo. Billy Gunz requested for him to meet him there. His phone rings as he walks through the gates.

"Yea."

"Meet him over by the lion's habitat. You know the rules." Missy disconnects the call. Baby Red checks the map that was given to him upon admission. He spots the lion's habitat west of him on the map. Making his way to Billy Gunz, he watched all the faces he passed by. He wondered if any of them were FEDs. What if Billy Gunz was setting him up?. His mind reeled with thoughts that didn't make sense but kept him aware of his surroundings. With his paranoia now sinking in he didn't know who to trust.

He reaches the lion's habitat. He sees Billy Gunz eating a bag of chips while admiring a huge lion with a thick brown mane. The lion sat proudly upon a boulder watching down on the other lions and lionesses wander around. Baby Red walked over and stood a few feet away from Billy Gunz.

"Look at him. The king of the jungle. The one that sits at the top of the food chain. There are only three animals that together could take him down. That's an elephant, fish, and a pig."

"How you figure?"

"The elephant with his big ears hear everything the lion says. The fish with his never blinking eyes sees everything the lion does. Together they tell the pig. And I'm sure you could guess what happens from there." Baby Red understood well the meaning behind his metaphor. "Without looking, how many people are in this area right now?"

"Seven. A family of four to my left. One zoo employee by the garbage can, and a young couple a few feet away holding hands looking at the lion cubs." Billy Gunz grins.

"I see that paranoia's kicked in. You finally see why it's a must a hustla on this level takes so many precautions. No matter if others see it as paranoia or not, it's how you stay safe in this game. I told you this level of the game ain't for everybody. It takes a special kind of man to hold the ground under his feet in these shoes. Some niggas ain't meant to be nothing more than a low to mid-level hustla."

"I might've run into a few problems, but I'm meant to wear those shoes." Billy Gunz laughs at that.

"Let's see, you got Ticky gunning for you, your girl in the hospital clinging to life, Wee Wee dead, Noodles and Pay Pay jumped ship, yo dope spots shot to hell, the feds after you. And not to mention you only have two days left to have my money. Boy, you got mo shit on yo ass than you can wipe. And you still believe you meant for these shoes?"

"I'm going to take care of Truth as soon -" Billy Gunz cut him off.

"Truth is the least of your worries. Since you ain't heard I'm going to put you on game. Truth tried to go out in a blaze of glory like yo boy Spooky did. But it didn't work out for him. He popped off a few cops then they let him have it. Pigs lit his ass up. Thirteen shots to the body and the nigga still lived. And that's the bad news for him. Because now he's in a wheelchair and shitting in a bag. And on top of all that he's going to spend the rest of his life in the joint like that. That goes to show death ain't always certain when you attempt suicide by cop, but the hell you receive after that is a promise."

"I'm sure you ain't just call me done here for a field trip and give me good news about Truth. So, what's the purpose of this meeting."

"What you in a rush?"

"Seeming I have less than forty-eight hours to come up with yo money, I would say so."

"I can respect that. I brought you here to let you know I need the rest of that work back you got left. I was trying to give you the opportunity to flip em like a real hustla and make back all the money of mines you lost. But with all this you got going on, the remainder of my dope that's in your possession is in jeopardy. I want you to drop it off to Missy at the car wash on 27th and Concordia at five o'clock tonight. And not a minute later."

"I'll be there."

"And Baby Red, don't try and skip town. I will find yo ass." Billy Gunz walks off snacking on his chips.

Baby Red and Do-Dirty sit in the car a block away from Ticky's house. He checks the time,11:07. "Dirt, we got less than six hours to go hit up Ticky's place and then run to the storage, grab the bricks, and be at the car wash. So, we got to find these bricks as fast as we can. I swear I hope those bricks are in that house."

"I'm telling you they got to be there. Even if Truth was the one holding them birds down, you know Ticky and went and grabbed them by now."

"I hope you're right. Because our lives are on the line."

"I hear you. But what you going to do about the FEDs though?"

"Let's worry about one thing at a time. I'll cross that bridge when I get to it. Right now, let's go get these bricks back." Do-Dirty grabs a box out the backseat. They hop out the car pulling their ski masks over their faces as they make their way to Ticky's house.

Do-Dirty creeps onto the porch and sits the box down and rings the doorbell. He hides in the nearby bushes next to Baby Red. "Who is it?" Dee Dee yells. Hearing no reply, she opens the door with the chopper around her neck as usual. She sees

149

nobody but hears a whimper at her feet. She looks down and sees two blue nose pitbull puppies in a box. "Aw, come here babies." She bends down and picks them up. Then turns around and yells in the house to Ticky. "Ticky look at these beautiful puppies!" Baby Red and Do-Dirty jump out the bushes putting their guns to her head before she could react.

"Let me get that up off you, baby," Do-Dirty tells her then takes the chopper off her neck.

"Where Ticky at?"

"I ain't telling you shit." Baby Red cocks back his gun and put it back to her head. "He's in the back."

"Walk!" Still, with puppies in hand, Dee Dee leads them into the house. Do-Dirty walked directly behind her with his gun to her head. Baby Red walked behind him. When they entered the living room, Do-Dirty didn't see Ms. Bitch chained to the wall near the entrance.

"Get em Ms. Bitch!" Dee Dee yells. Ms. Bitch jumps up and sinks her teeth into Do-Dirty's arm causing him to drop the gun. "Ticky!" Dee Dee screams as she runs through the living room. Baby Red delivers a shot to her thigh making her fall on the floor landing between the living room and dining room entrance. The puppies crawl from under her and scatter off.

Ticky was lying in bed watching TV when he heard Dee Dee scream his name followed by a gunshot. He grabs the sawed-off shotgun next to the bed and limped out of the room. He crept through the kitchen then into the dining room. He sees Dee Dee on the floor whining with a hole in her thigh. "Dee Dee, how many is it?" He whispers to her. She holds up two fingers. He moves closer to her and takes a quick look at her wound. "It's just a flesh wound you'll be alright." He hears the sound of Ms. Bitch with her jaws locked onto one of the niggas. Then he hears another shot and Ms. Bitch whimper.

Do-Dirty couldn't pry Ms. Bitch jaws off him as shook his arm like a play toy. Baby Red couldn't get a steady aim on her with Do-Dirty panicking trying to get her off of him. Dirt used his free hand and grabbed the gun from his waist. With much pain, he calmed himself and steadied his aim. Then when she stopped shaking his arm and just held her grip, he put a bullet in her head. He looked at the damage and seen a small chunk of meat was missing from his arm. It hurt like hell, but he wasted no time getting back to business. As he bent down to pick the chopper up Ticky came in.

"Ms. Bitch!!" He sees Ms. Bitch laid out on the floor with a bullet in her head. "You finna die now mothafucka," he says with tears in his eyes as he began busting off rounds from the gauge. He worked his way to the back as Baby Red bust a few shots off at him. He opens the basement door and makes a whistling sound. "Lucifer! Six! Get em!" Six and Lucifer come running out the basement like bats out of hell. They charged straight for the dining room where Do-Dirty and Baby Red were running into, while Ticky slips out the back door.

Lucifer runs towards Baby Red and Baby Red hits him with two shots to the chest and the one-eyed beast hits the floor with a whimper. Six growls with his eyes fixed on Baby Red. He jumps over the dining room table charging towards him. Baby Red shoot five shots into him, but he still didn't go down. He tries to shoot again, but his gun was out of bullets. Just before Six could sink his teeth into him, Do-Dirty let seven rounds spit out the chopper. All seven ripped through Six, he hit the ground and laid on his side breathing hard. Do-Dirty walks up to him and popped off four more shots sending six straight to hell.

Baby Red and Do-Dirty run to the back careful not to run into any more dogs and they see Ticky had slipped away. They walk back in the house and sees Dee Dee had made it to her feet and was hopping towards the front door. Baby Red grabs her before she could get to the door. "Where you going, bitch? Where the dope at?"

"In the back room."

"Lead the way. And if any more dogs pop out on us, I'm going to shoot yo ass again." She leads them to the back room and opens a safe that was installed in the floor. Inside was only one kilo and a few stacks of money. "Where the rest of the dope at?" Do-Dirty asks her.

"The rest of what dope? What you think you robbing the plug or something? This all we have!" Baby Red opens the kilo and taste it.

"Bitch, stop lying."

"Fuck! She ain't lying. This ain't our dope."

"You sure?"

"Yea I'm sure. I know the difference between straight drop and straight cut. This bullshit ain't ours." Baby Red tosses the kilo on the bed. Do-Dirty picks it back up.

"Well, we still taking it along with the money too. So, let me get that up out you too, baby." Dee Dee hands him the money and they bailout.

~ CHAPTER 19 ~

With so much heat on him, Baby Red and Do-Dirty sat inside a laundromat on the North Side of town to gather their thoughts. He checks the time. "Dirt it's 2:52. We need to get to the other side of town and get those bricks and that money out of storage."

"I know you ain't still considering returning the dope to this nigga," he says as he gets a soda out the vending machine.

"Hell nah. I ain't that kind of crazy. We ain't found that man's bricks or have the money to pay him back. To go give him the rest of the shit we have when I'm already a dead man would be stupid. We finna split all that shit up down the middle and leave town tonight. But it's going to be a challenge getting to that side of town with them people combing the streets for me." They both take a second to think.

"Then I'll go get them," he says popping open his can of soda.

"What?"

"So far, the police ain't looking for me. Everybody looking for you. It'll be safer for you to stay here and let me go get the bricks and money. Then I come back and scoop you and we leave town." He takes a sip of his soda.

"Nah, I don't know about that one."

"What other choice do you have? You too hot to be seen on that side of town. I'm sure every squad car in that area is riding around with your mugshot looking for you." Baby Red couldn't get around his logic. He looks Do-Dirty in the eye.

"Don't fuck me Dirt. Get those bricks and come back."

"We family nigga, I wouldn't do that to you. I'll be back." Baby Red hands him the key and the gate code to the storage. Do-Dirty hurries out the laundromat and pulls off in Baby Red's Charger. Baby Red hoped it was just his paranoia. But something in the pit of his stomach told him not to trust Do-Dirty to handle that mission.

"Three…five…nine…seven… Enter." Do-Dirty types in the code and the gate to the storage facility opens up. He looks at the paper and sees the storage unit he's looking for is H-11. He passes rows E and F then finds H, two lanes up. He turns right and a quarter of the way down, he spots unit 11 on his right side. He parks the car and pulls the key to the padlock out his back pocket. After getting the lock off, he lifts the storage door. Inside was a mattress, box spring, an older model big-screen television, and a few chairs. Baby Red didn't tell him exactly where in the storage the dope and money was.

Do-Dirty flips open the pocketknife on Baby Red's key chain and cut up the box spring and finds nothing. He moves on to the mattress, working hard to cut through the thick material with the dull blade that was in his hand. He cuts a small opening big enough to get a few fingers in, then rips it open with his hand and finds all his hard work was for nothing. "Shit! Where is it?" He looks around the small storage room and sees it was only one other logical place it could be.

He grabbed a screwdriver out the trunk. Then went over to the big screen television and began removing the back off of it. After removing several screws, he takes the back off and inside laid a duffle bag. Do-Dirty opened the bag and seen the ten bricks and racks of cash. A wide smile creased his face. He quickly zipped the bag back up and proceeded out of the storage room. As he put the bag in the trunk, his phone rang. He looked at the caller ID and seen it was Baby Red. He looked at the phone a moment as he debated the thoughts in his head. "Sorry cuz, it's my time to shine." He pressed the ignore button on the phone and slams the trunk close.

The time was 4:12 and Do-Dirty still wasn't back. Baby Red called his phone several times and got no answer. A bad feeling was growing in the pit of his stomach. If he wasn't out of town before that five o'clock meeting was to take place he was as good as dead.

An old man sweeping the floor in the laundromat turns up the volume on the TV to hear an episode of "Fresh Prince of Bel-Air" as he swept the floor. Everyone in the laundromat was watching the show. It was the episode where Will had lost to a pool shark and Uncle Phil had to come to his rescue with his pool skills. "Jeffrey, break out Lucille," Uncle Phil says. Jeffrey hands him the pool stick and just as Uncle Phil was about to do his thing the show was interrupted.

"Breaking news, police are looking for a man for questioning regarding a shootout at the Regency Motel in Madison and also several other shooting in Milwaukee." The news reporter posts a recent mugshot of Baby Red on the screen. "If you or someone you know have seen this man, Reddrick Walton, also known on the streets as Baby Red, please call authorities immediately. Don't try to approach him, he's considered to be armed and dangerous. There is a ten-thousand-dollar reward for any information that leads to his arrest. Now back to your regular scheduled programming."

All eyes fall on Baby Red. People started pulling out their phones. Baby Red dipped out of the laundromat and ran until he was far enough away. He tried dialing Do-Dirty, but it went straight to voicemail. He knew then Do-Dirty had played him.

It was 4:37 and he had to get out of town fast. A bus with the name Voices Of The Lord Gospel Choir written on it pulled into the parking lot of Popeye's Chicken. The people got out and went inside and Baby Red followed. He stood in line behind two of the women from the choir. "Did you hear that soprano they had in the Sacred Lamb's choir?"

"Gurl yea. That child sounded like a wounded duck." Baby Red listens a second as the two women discussed the choir competition they just left.

"Excuse me, ladies. I couldn't help but here y'all beautiful voices and accents. Where y'all from?"

"We from Douglasville, Georgia," the one to the left of him says.

"Really? I have a brother in Atlanta. I have been there a few times and love it out there."

"It ain't no place better than Georgia, honey."

"I agree with that. And judging by the looks of you beautiful sisters, I'd say God made some his best work out there," Baby Red says to win them over. The two women blushed.

"Honey, you'd betta slow down before I take you back to Georgia with me."

"I have been looking for a reason to go. Y'all wouldn't happen to have room on that bus for one more would you?"

"God always has room for another soul."

I guess it's true, God does look after fools and babies, Baby Red thought to himself.

After being treated to a meal of fried chicken, red beans, and rice and buttermilk biscuits they welcomed him aboard their tour bus. And just like that Baby Red was headed back to Georgia.

After ditching Baby Red's car, Do-Dirty checks into a motel on the West Side of town. He grins and rubs his hands together as he looks down at all the bricks and money laid out on the bed. "Yea, I'm in the money now, baby! That's right, I'm calling the shots now." His phone rings. Being so geeked up about his newfound wealth, he forgets to check the caller ID before answering. "Hello"

"Oh, so I see you ain't in jail. So that only means one thing. You ran off with the dope and money. You bitch ass nigga!"

Damn! Do-Dirty mouths to himself. Feeling already caught up he rolled with it. "Look at it from my point of view, Baby Red. You either going to prison when the FEDs catch you or to the grave when Billy Gunz catches you. So why shouldn't I inherit all the dope and money?" he says nonchalantly.

"I should've listened to Paris and let Truth kill yo ass."

"Yea well, should've, could've, would've, you know how that goes. But you take care and have a safe trip to hell," he says while counting the money on the bed.

"You better hope I don't find yo ass first." Baby Red disconnects the call. Do-Dirty shrugs his shoulders and tosses the phone on the bed. "He in his chest. Fuck that nigga and his feelings. I got money to make." Another call comes in. "What it do?"

"Do-Dirt with the work! What's going on nephew!"

"Eddie Cain this you?"

"You damn right nephew."

"What's up with you?"

"Man, just seeing if you heard what happened to Truth?"

"Yea, I heard. That lame got what he deserved."

"Well, if you heard, then why you ain't over here with that good dope of yours getting this money?"

"I still got to get rid of Ticky first so I can hustle in peace."

"If that's what's keeping you from bringing some of that A-1 back over these ways, then I got something that will help you get rid of Ticky for good."

"And what's that?"

"Meet me at Benny's bodega tomorrow and I'll give you just what you need."

Once in Georgia, Baby Red catches a ride to Atlanta from one of the choir members. He checks into a motel and thinks about what he's gonna do next. His funds were limited. With the FEDs on him, he needed to leave the country. But with only $490 to his name he barely had enough to leave the state. He had to make something shake. Georgia was only temporary. He couldn't stay there with the feds knowing he had links there.

With no work to hustle, he knew Billy Gunz would have to come see his plug soon. And by tomorrow being Sunday that just might be the day. Keeping that in mind, Baby Red came up with the only plan he could think of. He was going to rob the Mexican woman for the diaper bag. By doing so he knew he was playing with fire. And he also knew it wouldn't be easy. Especially not knowing if Billy Gunz would be there or not. But desperate times cause for desperate measures and Baby Red was beyond desperate.

He calls Shirley to get an update on Paris. She was stable but still in a coma. The doctors said since she'd made it through the last couple of nights, they had faith that she would recover. Once she did Baby Red was going to send for her. Hoping he'd be out of the country by then.

He wanted to reach out to Pay Pay and Noodles and even thought about reaching out to Classy. He thought he could really use an ally right then. But not knowing which of them, if not all three of them, ratted him out to the FEDs, he felt he was better off solo.

After a long hot shower and soaking in his thoughts, Baby Red laid back in bed. He closed his eyes to the world and hopes the light of tomorrow will end his nightmare.

~ CHAPTER 20 ~

Do-Dirty's phone has been blowing up since last night. He'd been hustling so hard that he hadn't been to sleep yet. That didn't matter to him. He was happy to be eating like a big dog. And the best part about everything was because he didn't pay for the work it was all profit.

The dope dating king chases his pleasure in the mouth of a young hype. Twenty-year-old Brittany, known on the West Side as the Head Queen, works him with her mouth. Do-Dirty head falls back, and he bites his lip as he reaches the peak of his excitement. He releases his pleasure all in her mouth. Brittany quickly spits it out with disgust. "Damn it Do-Dirty! I told you to tell me when you were about to cum. You know I don't like that shit in my mouth." Do-Dirty zips ups his pants and sparks up a cigarette.

"Go smoke that happy ending I just paid for and you'll be alright." A text comes in on his phone. The text read:

Eddie Cain: Where you at nephew?

It was from Eddie Cain. "I got to go, Brittany. We're definitely going to do this again though, real soon." Brittany gives him a thumbs up after taking a hit of her pipe.

Do-Dirty sits in the back of the musty bodega on the East Side of town watching the screen with Eddie Cain and Benny. "You see that? I told you, nephew, you'll knock him out the box with this one."

"More like put him in a box," Benny says with his thick Arab accent. Benny's real name was Mohammed Al'bin. But since there was already a Muhammad on the block everyone just started calling him Benny. He knew who sold dope in the hood, who robbed who, who killed who, and how they did it. Benny had dirt on everybody, but he never told shit. It was his way of forming an insurance policy with the hood. You don't fuck with him and he won't rat on you. When all the other stores in the neighborhood were getting robbed and vandalized, no one dared to touch Benny's bodega.

"Yea, let me get that," Do-Dirty says with excitement.

"You want this, I want let's say...three G's for it?"

"Three G's Benny?"

"Come on my friend. Could you really put a price on what you stand to gain from this?" The slick hustling Arab knew how to get anyone to pay the ridiculous prices he put on things. Whether it was a gallon of milk or a video that could put your enemy away for a long time.

"Fine Benny, three G's it is." Benny grinned as Do-Dirty counted out three G's into his hand. Benny ejects the disc from the DVD player and gives it to him.

"Pleasure doing business with you, Do-Dirty."

"You got something for me too, nephew?" Do-Dirty digs in his pants and pulls out a sixteenth for Eddie Cain.

Do-Dirty walks out of the store and walks towards his rental car parked towards the middle of the block. A man walked past holding a baby wrapped in a blanket. The man stops and turns around. "Do-Dirty, that's you?" Do-Dirty turns to see the man but doesn't recognize him.

"Who is you?"

"Don't worry about it." The blanket falls to the ground along with a baby doll, and in the man's hand was a 9mm Ruger. He let off four shots hitting Do-Dirty in the chest. He falls to the ground coughing up blood. The man comes up to him and grabs the disc out his hand.

"I'll take that. You know you one sloppy nigga. Don't you know a mothafucka is always watching? I mean, who leaves ten birds and cash in a ghetto ass motel room. Yea, I collected that. And to answer your question, I'm Billy Gunz and it was a pleasure to meet you, Do-Dirty. Now, let's say our good-byes."

BOOM! BOOM!

Billy Gunz put two more holes into Do-Dirty's chest. His body jerked up and down on the pavement as each shot hit him. His head falls to the side as blood flowed down the side of his mouth and his body goes limp. All the life in him left his body and Do-Dirty was dead.

Baby Red got to the church early. He wanted to be the first one there so he can see if Billy Gunz was going to be there, or if Missy came down today. He copped a dope fiend rental last night. It was a tinted-out Ford Taurus. He sat in the parking lot for over an hour before people started pulling in to attend service. Where he was parked, he could see everyone and every car that came in. After about a good thirty minutes, he finally seen the sign hope he hoped for. Missy's van comes pulling into the parking lot. She parks in her usual spot and got out with her kids. There was no sign of Billy Gunz. Baby Red thought about snatching the bag up from Missy as she walked into the church, but he knew that mission would be a failure. He wouldn't have enough time to get at her before she made it inside the church.

Fifteen minutes later, the Mexican woman pulls into the parking lot in a maroon-colored Jaguar. She parks near the front entrance. He pulls up to a spot closer to hers. His plan was to rob her for the bag as soon as she gets back to her car.

As he waited Baby Red turned the radio to the church's radio station. He was curious about what the preacher was preaching about today. A woman sings a beautiful version of Yolanda Adams's song "Open My Heart" that made Baby Red reflect on his life for a minute.

The woman finishes her solo and the Reverend began his sermon. "Let the church say Amen." The church says Amen in unison over the radio. "Church, God has put it on my heart today to preach this next sermon because somebody is in need of the blessing within this message. Amen?" The church says Amen. "I say somebody is in need of these words of the lord. I say somebody out there is in trouble. Somebody's life is in shambles. Somebody's headed for destruction. And that somebody needs to Stop! And hear the words of the lord. And the Lord says in Proverbs Chapter 10:2: Treasures of wickedness profit nothing: but righteousness delivereth from death... Then the Lord says in Chapter 12:15: The way of a fool is right in his own eyes: but he that hearkeneth onto counsel is wise... You still with me, church?" The church says Amen. "And then the lord says in Chapter 13:20: He that walketh with wise men shall be wise, but a companion of fools shall be destroyed..."

By the time the reverend finished up his sermon, Baby Red was more than convinced that today's message was for him. He turned the radio off, and church began to let out. Baby Red gets out his car leaving it started so he could make a quick getaway. He crouches down by his car. He was parked directly behind her Jaguar. Missy and her rug rats come out and get in their van and leave. A few minutes later, the Mexican woman comes walking out of the church. She stops in the front of the church to converse with a group of its members. She gave one of the men she was conversing with her keys. The man ran over and pulled her car around to her.

"Shit!" Baby Red says to himself. He couldn't let that money get away. It was his only ticket out of there and away from all his troubles.

He gets back into his car and follows her as she pulls off. She makes a left turn pulling out the parking lot. Then she went a little way down the road and got on the highway.

After following her on the highway for twenty minutes, she takes the next exit. She drives a short way down the street then pulls into a Wal-Mart parking lot. She parked in the middle of the lot and Baby Red took a spot a few cars away. He cocked back his gun and hopped out the car. As soon as the woman opened her car door and stepped out, Baby Red was right behind her with the gun to her head. "Give me the diaper bag and you won't get hurt." The woman stood there frozen for a second with her hands up. Then she let out a brief laugh.

"You were right. He fell for it."

"What?" he says with a look of confusion. Before he could turn around the van door behind him slid open and he was hit with the butt of a pistol. Everything went dark and Baby Red hit the ground.

He sat tied to a chair. His head was spinning, and his vision was blurry. He groaned from the pain of the blow he received to the back of the head. "It looks like our guest is finally coming to."

"Man, I had my money on this fool." He hears a familiar voice say. He tries to focus his eyes on the voices he heard around him. He blinks hard a couple of times and everything slowly started to come in focus.

"What I tell you, Joey Long? You're a bad judge of character." Baby Red sees Billy Gunz talking with Joey Long. Billy Gunz then turns his attention to him. "What's up kingpin? I thought I told you not to leave town. Damn you hardheaded. You can't even follow the rules of the game." Billy Gunz shakes his head at the shame. "Just a disobedient bastard ain't you." The Mexican woman walks into the room with a man.

"My mans, K Dolla. What up, baby?" Billy Gunz and Joey Long shake up with the man. Baby Red couldn't believe his eyes. It was Reverend Kevin Dollar. He walks over to Baby Red.

"Damn son, you really were going to rob my wife. You should've listened to the messages and warnings I was giving you in my sermons." Baby Red looks at him with a look that showed his mind trying to unravel the confusion.

"I take it by that confused look on your face you wondering what's going on. As usual, I'll put you on game. The three of us, along with many others from around the world, are members of the Black Order. I'm the chairman of the organization. We control all the drugs, amongst other things, from all over the world. You can consider us to be something like the Illuminati of the black market. You see, we set you up from the beginning. You fell for what we call the king's illusion. It's like a lil game we play to initiate new members. Joey Long here thought you had what it takes to be one of us. I had my money on someone else. So, we committed some minor infractions to get ourselves put in jail. I had Missy trail you to Minnesota and sic the cops on you. I knew with Baggy being dead you would come begging me to put you on. So, I put you on. Yet you still wasn't grateful. You wanted to meet the plug. Not knowing the whole time that I am the plug. I'm glad my money wasn't on you." Joey Long hands Billy Gunz a duffle bag full of money and then turns his attention to Baby Red.

"Baby Red, you cost me a lot of money man. I know you've seen me a few times following you in that tinted out Challenger. When I first started trailing you, I was proud of you. You were getting yo money like a real boss, but then you let that dumb ass cousin of yours be your downfall." He shakes his head at him. Baby Red's mind was spinning as everything started to unravel for him.

"If your money wasn't on me then who was it on?"

"Bring in our other guest," Billy Gunz tells Missy. A frown began to crease Baby Red's face as he sees who walks in. The man walks over and hands Billy Gunz a duffle bag. Billy Gunz opens it and shows Baby Red the missing kilos of dope. Baby Red was so heated he could've spit fire.

"You's bitch ass nigga, Pay Pay! You better hope these niggas kill me before I kill you! Whatever happened to loyalty?" Baby Red says, squirming to get loose from the chair he was tied to. Pay Pay turned to him.

"Nigga, you wasn't doing anything but leading us all to destruction. And as far as loyalty goes, to be loyal to a fool is to be loyal to foolishness, which makes you a fool in return." He turns to Billy Gunz. "I ain't a fool Billy Gunz. I learn to perfect myself by learning from the mistakes of the fools that make them."

"Answer this for us, youngin'. What would you have done if you got hit for those bricks?" K Dolla asks Pay Pay.

"Since the dope was so potent, I would've taken the remaining keys, some acetone, and a compressor and turned each brick into two. Then got my hustle on."

Billy Gunz smiles and swells with pride.

"I told y'all. I know a winner when I see one. I say we welcome him to The Order. All that agrees, say I." They all say I in unison and then welcome him into The Order.

"As your first order of business, what you suggest we do with him?" Billy Gunz asks, pointing to Baby Red.

"I got something for him. Ain't that right, baby." Baby Red turns and sees Noodles walking up behind him. Before he could say anything, she put a rag filled with chloroform over his face. Seconds later, he was out.

Baby Red hears the sound of several sirens blaring as he starts to come to. He sees he's back in his motel room and couldn't help but wonder if it was all just a dream. The knot on his head told him it wasn't. As he gets up, he feels something wet on his hand and sees that it's blood. He sees a knife in his other hand. He looked behind him to find the source of all the blood. He sees Classy laid there with her throat cut open and eyes to the ceiling. His eyes grow wide with shock. His phone rings. "Hello"

"Rise and shine superstar. You all over the news. Take a look outsides" Billy Gunz tells him. Baby Red goes to the window and sees several squad cars, FBI, and news crews outside of his motel room. Panic set in. He sees his gun lying on the nightstand and grabs it. He tries to take cover underneath the windowsill. "A dead federal witness in yo bed? Not a good look. Ain't no way out of this one. You could try the blaze of glory thing, but you see how that worked out for Truth."

"Like you told me in jail, there's always a way out." Baby Red puts the gun to his head and BOOM! Game over.

~ CHAPTER 21 ~

Terry gets up to answer the door. She looks out the peephole and sees a UPS worker standing on the porch. She opens the door. "Can I help you?"

"I have a delivery for a Ms. Terry Michelle."

"That's me," Terry says surprised to be getting a package. She signs for the cardboard envelope then closes the door. She quickly opens it up and sees it's just a DVD. She smacks her lips. She was hoping it was some money or something she could exchange for some dope. She walks into the living room where Ticky was playing with the blue nose puppies. The pups chased a towel he dragged across the floor. "Ticky, let me use yo DVD player. I want to check the DVD out I just got."

"Go in my room and watch it."

"Okay." Terry grabs a bag of popcorn and walks to the back room. She turns the TV on and slides the DVD in.

"Oh, that's the old block. This got to be an old video though because Mr. Davis house ain't there no mo. That house burned down two or three years ago," she says to herself, recognizing the video is from the past. As she chews her popcorn, she sees something that grips her heart. She sees herself coming home from nursing school. Her daughter, Erica, runs up to her and gives her a hug. Terry picks her up and whirls her around and smothers her with kisses. Tears race down Terry's cheeks as she watches. She then sees herself go into the house while Erica stayed on the porch playing. Then she sees the new niggas on the block talking to Truth and Ticky. A man pulls out a gun and they all started shooting. Terry puts her hands over her mouth when she sees what happens next. Ticky comes down the street busting. Erica bends down to pick up a toy. Ticky sends a shot her way and Erica falls to the ground holding her neck. Not being able to handle watching anymore, she turns the TV off. She couldn't believe that Ticky was the one responsible for Erica's death. The one who was responsible for her having to stay high so she wouldn't have to keep seeing those images in her head. The images of Erica choking on her own blood and the lifeless stare that was left in her eyes.

Ticky was still playing with the puppies when she walked to the living room. He had his back to her, but heard her walk in. "You finished that movie already? Or was it that weak?" he says before hearing the cocking of a shotgun. He turns around slowly and sees Terry standing there holding his Mossberg pump with tears in her eyes. Seeing the pain in her eyes he knew what it was about. He knew it couldn't be but one thing on that disc that would make her turn against him like this. And somehow, he knew this day would come.

"I'm sorry, Terry." She shakes her head.

"Sorry won't bring my baby back." She pulls the trigger and the kickback from the blast pushes her back a couple of feet, but she still manages to hit Ticky in the chest. Making him fall over the couch dead with a golf ball size hole in his chest.

To Be Continued...
Nightmares of a Hustla 2
Coming Soon

Submission Guideline

Submit the first three chapters of your completed manuscript to ldpsubmissions@gmail.com, subject line: Your book's title. The manuscript must be in a .doc file and sent as an attachment. Document should be in Times New Roman, double spaced and in size 12 font. Also, provide your synopsis and full contact information. If sending multiple submissions, they must each be in a separate email.

Have a story but no way to send it electronically? You can still submit to LDP/Ca$h Presents. Send in the first three chapters, written or typed, of your completed manuscript to:

LDP: Submissions Dept
Po Box 944
Stockbridge, Ga 30281

DO NOT send original manuscript. Must be a duplicate.

Provide your synopsis and a cover letter containing your full contact information.

Thanks for considering LDP and Ca$h Presents.

<u>Coming Soon from Lock Down Publications/Ca$h Presents</u>

BOW DOWN TO MY GANGSTA

By **Ca$h**

TORN BETWEEN TWO

By **Coffee**

THE STREETS STAINED MY SOUL **II**

By **Marcellus Allen**

BLOOD OF A BOSS **VI**

SHADOWS OF THE GAME II

By **Askari**

LOYAL TO THE GAME **IV**

By **T.J. & Jelissa**

A DOPEBOY'S PRAYER **II**

By **Eddie "Wolf" Lee**

IF LOVING YOU IS WRONG… **III**

By **Jelissa**

TRUE SAVAGE **VII**

MIDNIGHT CARTEL III

DOPE BOY MAGIC IV

CITY OF KINGZ II

By **Chris Green**

BLAST FOR ME **III**

A SAVAGE DOPEBOY III

CUTTHROAT MAFIA III

By **Ghost**

A HUSTLER'S DECEIT III

KILL ZONE **II**

BAE BELONGS TO ME III

A DOPE BOY'S QUEEN III

By **Aryanna**

COKE KINGS V

KING OF THE TRAP II

By **T.J. Edwards**

GORILLAZ IN THE BAY V

De'Kari

THE STREETS ARE CALLING II

Duquie Wilson

KINGPIN KILLAZ IV

STREET KINGS III

PAID IN BLOOD III

CARTEL KILLAZ IV

DOPE GODS III

Hood Rich

SINS OF A HUSTLA II

ASAD

KINGZ OF THE GAME V

Playa Ray

SLAUGHTER GANG IV

RUTHLESS HEART IV

By **Willie Slaughter**

THE HEART OF A SAVAGE III

By **Jibril Williams**

FUK SHYT II

By Blakk Diamond

THE REALEST KILLAZ III

By Tranay Adams

TRAP GOD III

By Troublesome

YAYO IV

A SHOOTER'S AMBITION III

By S. Allen

GHOST MOB

Stilloan Robinson

KINGPIN DREAMS III

By Paper Boi Rari

CREAM II

By Yolanda Moore

SON OF A DOPE FIEND III

By Renta

FOREVER GANGSTA II

GLOCKS ON SATIN SHEETS III

By Adrian Dulan

LOYALTY AIN'T PROMISED II

By Keith Williams

THE PRICE YOU PAY FOR LOVE II

By Destiny Skai

CONFESSIONS OF A GANGSTA II

By Nicholas Lock

I'M NOTHING WITHOUT HIS LOVE II

By Monet Dragun

LIFE OF A SAVAGE IV

A GANGSTA'S QUR'AN II

MURDA SEASON II

GANGLAND CARTEL II

By **Romell Tukes**

QUIET MONEY III

THUG LIFE II

By **Trai'Quan**

THE STREETS MADE ME III

By **Larry D. Wright**

THE ULTIMATE SACRIFICE VI

IF YOU CROSS ME ONCE II

ANGEL III

By **Anthony Fields**

THE LIFE OF A HOOD STAR

By Ca$h & Rashia Wilson

FRIEND OR FOE II

By **Mimi**

SAVAGE STORMS II

By **Meesha**

BLOOD ON THE MONEY II

By J-Blunt

THE STREETS WILL NEVER CLOSE II

By K'ajji

NIGHTMARES OF A HUSTLA II

By King Dream

King Dream

Available Now

RESTRAINING ORDER **I & II**
By **CA$H & Coffee**
LOVE KNOWS NO BOUNDARIES **I II & III**
By **Coffee**
RAISED AS A GOON I, II, III & IV
BRED BY THE SLUMS I, II, III
BLAST FOR ME I & II
ROTTEN TO THE CORE I II III
A BRONX TALE I, II, III
DUFFEL BAG CARTEL I II III IV
HEARTLESS GOON I II III IV
A SAVAGE DOPEBOY I II
HEARTLESS GOON I II III
DRUG LORDS I II III
CUTTHROAT MAFIA I II
By **Ghost**
LAY IT DOWN **I & II**
LAST OF A DYING BREED
BLOOD STAINS OF A SHOTTA I & II III
By **Jamaica**
LOYAL TO THE GAME I II III
LIFE OF SIN I, II III
By **TJ & Jelissa**
BLOODY COMMAS I & II
SKI MASK CARTEL I II & III

174

KING OF NEW YORK I II,III IV V

RISE TO POWER I II III

COKE KINGS I II III IV

BORN HEARTLESS I II III IV

KING OF THE TRAP

By **T.J. Edwards**

IF LOVING HIM IS WRONG…I & II

LOVE ME EVEN WHEN IT HURTS I II III

By **Jelissa**

WHEN THE STREETS CLAP BACK I & II III

THE HEART OF A SAVAGE I II

By **Jibril Williams**

A DISTINGUISHED THUG STOLE MY HEART I II & III

LOVE SHOULDN'T HURT I II III IV

RENEGADE BOYS I II III IV

PAID IN KARMA I II III

SAVAGE STORMS

By **Meesha**

A GANGSTER'S CODE I &, II III

A GANGSTER'S SYN I II III

THE SAVAGE LIFE I II III

CHAINED TO THE STREETS I II III

BLOOD ON THE MONEY

By J-Blunt

PUSH IT TO THE LIMIT

By **Bre' Hayes**

BLOOD OF A BOSS **I, II, III, IV, V**

SHADOWS OF THE GAME

By **Askari**

THE STREETS BLEED MURDER **I, II & III**

THE HEART OF A GANGSTA I II& III

By **Jerry Jackson**

CUM FOR ME I II III IV V

An **LDP Erotica Collaboration**

BRIDE OF A HUSTLA **I II & II**

THE FETTI GIRLS **I, II& III**

CORRUPTED BY A GANGSTA I, II III, IV

BLINDED BY HIS LOVE

THE PRICE YOU PAY FOR LOVE

DOPE GIRL MAGIC I II III

By **Destiny Skai**

WHEN A GOOD GIRL GOES BAD

By **Adrienne**

THE COST OF LOYALTY I II III

By Kweli

A GANGSTER'S REVENGE **I II III & IV**

THE BOSS MAN'S DAUGHTERS I II III IV V

A SAVAGE LOVE **I & II**

BAE BELONGS TO ME I II

A HUSTLER'S DECEIT I, II, III

WHAT BAD BITCHES DO I, II, III

SOUL OF A MONSTER I II III

KILL ZONE

A DOPE BOY'S QUEEN I II

Nightmares of a Hustla

By **Aryanna**

A KINGPIN'S AMBITON

A KINGPIN'S AMBITION **II**

I MURDER FOR THE DOUGH

By **Ambitious**

TRUE SAVAGE I II III IV V VI

DOPE BOY MAGIC I, II, III

MIDNIGHT CARTEL I II

CITY OF KINGZ

By **Chris Green**

A DOPEBOY'S PRAYER

By **Eddie "Wolf" Lee**

THE KING CARTEL **I, II & III**

By **Frank Gresham**

THESE NIGGAS AIN'T LOYAL **I, II & III**

By **Nikki Tee**

GANGSTA SHYT **I II &III**

By **CATO**

THE ULTIMATE BETRAYAL

By **Phoenix**

BOSS'N UP **I , II & III**

By **Royal Nicole**

I LOVE YOU TO DEATH

By Destiny J

I RIDE FOR MY HITTA

I STILL RIDE FOR MY HITTA

By **Misty Holt**

177

LOVE & CHASIN' PAPER

By **Qay Crockett**

TO DIE IN VAIN

SINS OF A HUSTLA

By **ASAD**

BROOKLYN HUSTLAZ

By **Boogsy Morina**

BROOKLYN ON LOCK I & II

By **Sonovia**

GANGSTA CITY

By **Teddy Duke**

A DRUG KING AND HIS DIAMOND I & II III

A DOPEMAN'S RICHES

HER MAN, MINE'S TOO I, II

CASH MONEY HO'S

By Nicole Goosby

TRAPHOUSE KING **I II & III**

KINGPIN KILLAZ I II III

STREET KINGS I II

PAID IN BLOOD **I II**

CARTEL KILLAZ I II III

DOPE GODS I II

By **Hood Rich**

LIPSTICK KILLAH **I, II, III**

CRIME OF PASSION I II & III

FRIEND OR FOE

By **Mimi**

STEADY MOBBN' **I, II, III**

THE STREETS STAINED MY SOUL

By **Marcellus Allen**

WHO SHOT YA **I, II, III**

SON OF A DOPE FIEND I II

Renta

GORILLAZ IN THE BAY **I II III IV**

TEARS OF A GANGSTA I II

DE'KARI

TRIGGADALE I II III

Elijah R. Freeman

GOD BLESS THE TRAPPERS I, II, III

THESE SCANDALOUS STREETS I, II, III

FEAR MY GANGSTA I, II, III IV, V

THESE STREETS DON'T LOVE NOBODY I, II

BURY ME A G I, II, III, IV, V

A GANGSTA'S EMPIRE I, II, III, IV

THE DOPEMAN'S BODYGAURD I II

THE REALEST KILLAZ I II

Tranay Adams

THE STREETS ARE CALLING

Duquie Wilson

MARRIED TO A BOSS... I II III

By Destiny Skai & Chris Green

KINGZ OF THE GAME I II III IV

Playa Ray

SLAUGHTER GANG I II III

RUTHLESS HEART I II III

By Willie Slaughter

FUK SHYT

By Blakk Diamond

DON'T F#CK WITH MY HEART I II

By Linnea

ADDICTED TO THE DRAMA I II III

By Jamila

YAYO I II III

A SHOOTER'S AMBITION I II

By S. Allen

TRAP GOD I II

By Troublesome

FOREVER GANGSTA

GLOCKS ON SATIN SHEETS I II

By Adrian Dulan

TOE TAGZ I II III

By Ah'Million

KINGPIN DREAMS I II

By Paper Boi Rari

CONFESSIONS OF A GANGSTA

By Nicholas Lock

I'M NOTHING WITHOUT HIS LOVE

By Monet Dragun

CAUGHT UP IN THE LIFE I II III

By Robert Baptiste

NEW TO THE GAME I II III

By **Malik D. Rice**

LIFE OF A SAVAGE I II III

A GANGSTA'S QUR'AN

MURDA SEASON

GANGLAND CARTEL

By **Romell Tukes**

LOYALTY AIN'T PROMISED

By **Keith Williams**

QUIET MONEY I II

THUG LIFE

By **Trai'Quan**

THE STREETS MADE ME I II

By **Larry D. Wright**

THE ULTIMATE SACRIFICE I, II, III, IV, V

KHADIFI

IF YOU CROSS ME ONCE

ANGEL I II

By **Anthony Fields**

THE LIFE OF A HOOD STAR

By **Ca$h & Rashia Wilson**

THE STREETS WILL NEVER CLOSE

By **K'ajji**

CREAM

By **Yolanda Moore**

NIGHTMARES OF A HUSTLA

By **King Dream**

BOOKS BY LDP'S CEO, CA$H

TRUST IN NO MAN

TRUST IN NO MAN 2

TRUST IN NO MAN 3

BONDED BY BLOOD

SHORTY GOT A THUG

THUGS CRY

THUGS CRY 2

THUGS CRY 3

TRUST NO BITCH

TRUST NO BITCH 2

TRUST NO BITCH 3

TIL MY CASKET DROPS

RESTRAINING ORDER

RESTRAINING ORDER 2

IN LOVE WITH A CONVICT

LIFE OF A HOOD STAR

Coming Soon

BONDED BY BLOOD 2

BOW DOWN TO MY GANGSTA

Nightmares of a Hustla

CPSIA information can be obtained
at www.ICGtesting.com
Printed in the USA
LVHW020111101220
673729LV00014B/1502

9 781952 936517